My Feline Protector

Middlemarch Shifters 6

Shelley Munro

My Feline Protector

Print ISBN: 978-1-99-106307-6
Digital ISBN: 978-0-473-35748-1

Editor: Mary Moran

Cover: Kim Killion, Killion Group, Inc.

Munro Press, New Zealand.

First Munro Press electronic publication July 2016

First Munro Press print publication December 2022

For Paul.

Introduction

A glimpse across a crowded room...

Feline shapeshifter Gerard Drummond catches sight of a human woman with innocent eyes and lush curves and he's toast. He desperately wants to meet her, and with his best friend Henry as his wingman, he's soon chatting with the gorgeous London Allbright and her sister Jenny.

Despite swearing off men, the sexy Middlemarch local charms London, and she agrees to take part in a zombie run, even though she isn't athletic in the least. The longer she spends with Gerard, the more she's tempted, but no...she's heading back to England and has no time for romance.

The obstacles aren't only on the zombie run course.

Gerard can't let London leave, and now it seems Henry is hitting it off with London's sister. There must be a way...

A shocking murder changes everything and throws their lives into turmoil. Gerard and London, Henry, and Jenny. Nothing will ever be the same as danger stalks London, and Gerard struggles to keep his English beauty safe.

Warning: Contains a sexy feline male who knows exactly who he wants and isn't afraid to chase her, to woo her, to protect and love her until she decides to stop running.

Chapter 1

Meeting the Locals

"Those two guys are staring at us." Jenny Weaver giggled, a faint blush creeping into her lightly tanned cheeks. "They're cute. Have you noticed the guys around here are big and e-excellent eye candy?" She hiccupped, after too many glasses of wine to celebrate their successful four-day journey along the rail trail.

London Allbright hid her grin behind a glass of wine, but didn't turn her head to search out the men in the low lighting of the country pub. It was good to see her older sister happy again, and she was glad she'd succumbed to Jenny's pleas to holiday in New Zealand and Australia.

They'd both needed the break from the harsh English winter, Jenny most of all. The shenanigans of Jenny's husband, soon to be ex, had battered her sister, left her a shadow of her normal confident self. It was pleasing to see her return.

"Hello, ladies. Would you take pity on us and share your table? It's busy in here tonight."

London forgot herself and gaped at the two men. The one who spoke was tall with black hair and green eyes that sparkled with fun. His wicked grin held more sex appeal than was good for a man and took him to drool-worthy. With his broad chest and runner's build, he grabbed attention, despite his casual shirt and faded blue jeans.

"Of course you can," Jenny said before London could reply.

"I'm Gerard Drummond." He gestured at the other man. "My friend Henry Anderson."

The two men pulled out chairs and sat with their drinks. Gerard's friend was big and solid, much beefier and his dark blond hair was longer. London glanced at her sister and forced herself not to grin. Jenny couldn't take her eyes off Henry. Ogling was the word.

"I'm Jenny Weaver and my sister London Allbright," Jenny said.

Jenny's perky attitude thrilled her, even if she did worry about Jenny going too far. *Prude*. At least that was what Jenny had called her when she'd expressed her concerns and suggested moving slower with the men they'd met during their holiday. Seize the day or night as the case may be, according to Jenny.

Royce had—no, she wouldn't waste a thought on her brother-in-law. The man was a bully and not worth the effort. Jenny intended to set divorce proceedings in motion and was considering moving to Bath after living in West London for many years.

"Ah, a sexy accent." Gerard patted his chest near his heart.

Jenny smiled. "I live in West London and my sister is from Bath."

"It's busy in here tonight," London said, eyeing the number of customers waiting for service at the bar. The dining area was also doing a roaring trade, and the scent of blue cod and chips had her stomach rumbling. "Is there something on?"

"It's the zombie run tomorrow and the craft market," Gerard said. "Haven't you seen the posters around the town?"

"Ah, I saw the posters," London said.

A bark interrupted, and she stared around in surprise.

"Oh, what a cute little dog," Jenny said.

"Geoffrey," Henry said in a gruff voice and clicked his fingers. The small terrier trotted to Henry and sat beside him. "He's not meant to be in here."

"They won't notice with this crowd," Gerard said. "Now that he knows where you are, he'll sit under the table."

Henry nodded and crouched to speak to his dog. To London's amazement, the white-and-black dog went under the table and sprawled out to wait.

"How long are you staying?" Gerard asked.

London smiled. "We've booked for two nights. Neither of us are cyclists and we weren't sure how sore we'd feel once we finished cycling the rail trail."

"Do you have sore muscles?" Henry asked, his gaze darting to Jenny.

"Not as bad as we thought," Jenny said.

The two men exchanged a quick glance. "We're looking for two women to join our team in the zombie run. I don't suppose we could persuade you to help us out?"

London opened her mouth to say, *hell no*. She wasn't a runner.

Jenny spoke first. "We'd love to. I've always wanted to enter a zombie run. Something different and fun."

Gerard sipped his beer, his gaze on London. "You'd be helping us out of a jam. We'd lined up two women to join our team, but one is sick and the other stayed in Wellington."

"I'm not much of a runner," London said, but she weakened under her sister's pleading stare. Before this holiday she hadn't known she could bungee jump or cycle for days either.

Gerard placed his hand on her arm, the heat sending an unexpected frisson skipping across her skin. "Please consider it."

Her sister was chatting with Henry, obviously considering their plans for tomorrow fixed. Although she was pleased to see the return of her bubbly sister, she hadn't missed her managing side. Big sister bossy syndrome. She sighed. "My sister talked me into a bungee jump. I thought I might wet myself," she confessed. "I can't believe a zombie run is any worse. Okay. I'm in, and I'll do my best, but I've never been big on exercise." She gestured at her curves and wrinkled her nose. "I'm more at home in an office, and my hobby is cooking. On my most exciting days, I visit historical properties, so I'm not promising great things."

The rumble of Gerard's laugh tugged at her, and her gaze flew to his. Something in this man called to her, heck, enticed her to reckless behavior. She sipped her wine and forced her gaze off his smiley face, concentrating instead on the skinny, stooped man collecting empty glasses from a nearby table.

"This race is about fun and participation. We're raising funds for the community. The craft market is also this weekend. They're holding the race in the morning and opening the market in the afternoon."

"That's more my speed," London said, her focus right back on the hunk.

"I'll escort you around the market. I know the best vendors. The ladies head for the clothing stall run by Isabella Mitchell. You might need protection. They had a violent squabble over a dress last month."

London stared, unsure if he was telling the truth. "Are you telling fibs?"

He angled his body toward hers, fans of tiny crinkles appearing at the corners of his eyes. "Honest. I had to help Leo Mitchell break up the fight. How long are you spending in New Zealand?"

"We're catching the train to Dunedin the day after tomorrow and picking up a hire car to drive along the coast to Christchurch. Jenny wants to swim with dolphins and I want to go whale watching. We're making our way to Picton, catching the ferry over to Wellington, then flying home."

A phone chimed behind her, and one of the three guys at the nearest table slammed the flat of his palm onto the polished wood to emphasize his point, snaring her attention for a second.

"Sounds good. Have you visited Auckland?"

"We spent a few days in Auckland at the start of our holiday, visited Rotorua and Taupo. You live in a beautiful country."

"We do," Gerard said.

"Do you live in Middlemarch?" She wrinkled her nose as a group of newcomers wound through the tables by them and started to breathe through her mouth to combat the stench of body odor. Someone needed to bathe.

"Yes, but Henry and I are newcomers. We've purchased a property and are starting a security business. Originally, we wanted to base ourselves in Christchurch to be near our friend, but property is in short supply after the earthquake. Sam, our friend, suggested Middlemarch since he and his wife grew up here."

Music started and the crowd in the bustling pub cheered.

"They have a band for tonight and tomorrow," Gerard explained. "Gives me an excuse to ask you to dance, see how we'll fit."

Henry rose and held out his hand to Jenny. Her sister curled her fingers around Henry's and let him lead her to the dancefloor with not a word spoken. The non-verbal cues, however, made London blush and want to fan her face. She turned back to Gerard with no idea of what to say, given that he'd witnessed the crackle of sensual electricity between the pair. London never jumped into bed with a man so fast, preferring to get to know them first, but he might have received a different impression after seeing Jenny with his friend.

Gerard winked at London Allbright, the blush that crawled over her creamy skin charming him. Instead of dancing straightaway, he was content to chat and get to know her better. God, she was sexy, enticing, and his feline agreed because he hadn't ceased his inner purring since they'd joined the women. He'd seen them across the crowded pub and without a word to Henry, he'd started over to their table. He'd heard Henry's soft curse, his grumble, but his best friend didn't seem so put out now. Easy to see Henry liked Jenny, London's sister, which worked well for both of them.

He caught London's glance at Jenny and Henry, the curve of her plump pink lips and the sparkle of her blue eyes. She'd pulled her glossy brown hair into one of those high ponytails that whacked a man in the face if he wasn't alert. He itched to tug off the purple thing holding it tight and run his fingers through the perfumed strands.

"So, how was the bike ride? Henry and I were discussing cycling part of the path once we have free time."

"The first day—I thought I might croak," she said in a dry voice. "A hot bath and a few drinks helped me feel better. The second day, I walked like a duck. Another hot bath, liniment and dinner and drinks at a historical pub helped ease the pain. I didn't want to cycle on the third day but Jenny dragged me out, and it wasn't too bad. The scenery is gorgeous, the weather was kind. The fourth day, I enjoyed but was glad to finish."

Her self-deprecating humor made his lips curve and her crisp English accent put the seal on his initial attraction.

"After the race and our market visit, I promise to ply you with drinks."

"There won't be a hot bath. The bed-and-breakfast only has a shower."

"We have one big enough for two." Gerard's feline let out an extra loud purr as he imagined sharing the bath with this beauty. "You can use it and I'll throw in a massage. What do you say?"

"A massage? Are you any good?"

Gerard flexed his fingers. "I am a master." Not a lie. He'd gone out with a physical therapist a few years ago, and she'd taught him a thing or two. A man could never have too many skills.

Her smile lit her face, and Gerard was toast. He'd laughed at Sam Mitchell when he said he knew Lisa was his mate from a young age. Gerard hadn't believed a word of Sam's certainty. One look and a few minutes with London Allbright had changed his tune. He and his feline were in complete agreement. Now all he had to do was work with the time he had and convince London to his way of thinking.

Difficult but not impossible.

"Tell me about this security business. I wouldn't have thought there'd be much business in the country."

"We're not far from Queenstown and Wanaka. Lots of people have luxury homes and holiday getaways. Property is in hot demand since the *Lord of the Rings* movies. We're close to Dunedin, so we have a large pool of leads for our business."

"Why security?"

"Henry and I were both in the army. We wanted to use the skills we learned there."

"What services will you be offering?" She sounded interested, something Gerard found unusual in the women he met in pubs and other pick-up spots. It made him like her even more.

"We intend to offer full-site security. Security for buildings and properties. Security for people and computers. Data protection is big business these days. That's Henry's specialty."

"That's a lot for two men to cover."

Astute lady. "Yes. We intend to start small, and we have army friends we can recruit when we get busier." He sipped his beer, the condensation of the glass wet against his palm. "You work in an office?"

"Yes, secretary and personal assistant. It's easy to get a job in this field if you're a good worker. It's why I didn't hesitate too long when it came to taking time off my current job to come with Jenny when she said she needed a change of scenery."

"She's been sick?"

"No." London hesitated, deliberating on what to tell him. "Problems with her marriage," she said finally. "She made the separation legal and intends to start divorce proceedings on our return."

"No chance of a reconciliation?"

She shook her head, and Gerard changed the subject. "Want to dance?"

13

Her face brightened, and she grinned, making him realize she had two cute dimples. "I am an excellent dancer."

Gerard stood, scooting his chair over the wooden floor. "Is that so? I'm not bad myself." He reached for her hand, and she didn't hesitate to slip her fingers into his. The physical contact had his breath catching. His nostrils flared as he tugged her closer and inhaled her scent—something floral with a hint of spiciness that a man might wear. Yet another contradiction. He had paid little attention to her clothing, but he saw she was wearing a dress with a full skirt that hit her above the knee. It was pretty and feminine and made the most of her sexy curves. Perfect for dancing.

He swung her into his arms and started a foxtrot to test her abilities. She fell into step without faltering, following his lead.

"This is a treat."

Her eyes sparkled. "It is. Where did you learn to dance?"

"My parents were in to ballroom dancing, and they dragged me and my younger sister along to lessons. I fought learning until I realized it was great for meeting girls. You?"

"I learned for a friend's wedding and found I enjoyed dancing. I kept up the lessons." She glanced past his right shoulder, her friendly countenance freezing for a brief second. Gerard caught her as she misstepped, saw the flash of fear, the uncertainty, followed by a release of the tension in her shoulders.

"You all right?"

"What?" She shook her head, almost as if she were shaking off a problem. Then, she focused on him. "Sorry. I thought I saw someone I knew."

"Did you?"

"Pardon?"

"Did you see someone you know? We can say hello."

"No. It wasn't...I mean, there was a resemblance." She gave a light laugh, but didn't quite pull it off. "They say everyone has a doppelgänger, don't they? For a moment this man looked like someone at home. But it wasn't him. Just a passing resemblance."

The man had frightened her. The tone of her voice—expressionless yet precise—indicated something lurking beneath the surface, something hidden and painful. Gerard scanned the crowd, his feline on the defensive. He didn't intercept a gaze out of place, apart from two of his feline acquaintances eyeing up London. He bared his teeth at them, narrowed his eyes, relaxing only when they laughingly gave way to his visual commands.

The music changed to something faster, more modern.

"Let's see if you know this one." Gerard moved into jive steps, and to his delight, she followed again without hesitation, even the tricky, showier moves. He spun and twirled her, dipped and then tossed her between his legs. The surrounding crowd withdrew to watch and *oohed* and *aahed*, then clapped with a thunderous applause at the song's close.

"No more," London said. "If you want to drag me past zombies tomorrow, you will have to let me rest."

"That was fun." His heart still beat fast, and he was eager to learn more. Asking about her journey and the things the girls had seen sounded a safe bet to start.

Their table was empty when he led her back, and he glanced around to see Henry still on the dance floor with Jenny.

He handed her the remains of her wine, and she frowned at it.

"I'll buy a new glass," she said.

Gerard with his mind on his next move was slower to understand. He sniffed his beer before his mind caught up. "You're worried someone might have put something in your drink."

"It pays to be careful. One of my friends... Never mind. Can I get you another beer?"

"You're right to be careful, but this is one pub, one town where you never have to worry. I'll get your drink. Which wine are you drinking?"

"I'll get it," she said, staring at him.

Fuck. She thought he might stick something in her drink. His feline's growl rumbled through his mind, incensed at the lack of trust. He forced back his protest and nodded. "Will you get me a lager?" He pulled out his wallet and handed her a twenty-dollar note.

Henry and Jenny returned while London was getting drinks. Henry's arm remained around Jenny's waist, and his friend looked mighty cozy. Pleased with himself. "Jenny and I are going for a walk, then we're going to our place."

Gerard's brows rose. Quick work, even for Henry.

"London has gone for drinks."

"Can you tell her we're going?" Jenny asked.

"I'd prefer it if you'd wait until she brings the drinks, so you can tell her yourself. I don't want her to think Henry kidnapped you."

"Pooh," Jenny said and wrinkled her nose.

Pooh? Gerard's brows rose again, this time his attention on Henry. His friend gave him a lazy grin. Hell, both of them reeked of desire. No matter what London said to her sister, this vehicle was already in gear. There was no way these two wouldn't end up fucking each other silly tonight.

"Ah, London." Jenny beamed at her sister, her blue eyes shining with excitement, her breathing faster than normal.

Gerard angled his body away a fraction, so his feline didn't receive as much of the lusty fallout between his werewolf buddy and his new lady.

"Henry and I are leaving."

"But we've just got another drink," London protested.

Jenny laughed, a blush creeping into her cheeks. She was attractive with her light brown hair and trim figure, but she bore a look of fragility her sister didn't possess. She leaned toward London and whispered in her ear. Gerard hid his amusement as London's mouth rounded, and she glanced at Henry. Color bloomed in her cheeks as she stepped away from her sister.

"Okay." London's voice shook a fraction. "I'll see you in the morning."

Gerard could tell she wanted to say more but his presence, Henry's presence, stilled her tongue.

Henry and Jenny left with Geoffrey trotting behind the couple. An uncomfortable silence remained in their wake.

"Are you going to Australia again when you leave New Zealand?"

"Our flight goes via Sydney, and we're stopping off for a few days. Jenny wants to see a show at the Sydney Opera House and to do the bridge climb."

"How are you with heights?"

London smiled, and her pretty eyes lit from within, as if she were laughing at herself. "I close my eyes and pretend I'm on the ground. Jenny assures me the bridge climb is safe, but my knees will knock like castanets the entire time. I'll try to get out of it, but Jenny is the bossy older sister. Somehow, she always gets her way."

"You're not as intrepid as your sister."

"That's not a bad thing."

"I didn't say that." Gerard reached for her hand on instinct, and when their fingers twined, it felt right. He liked this woman. A lot. "I get the impression your sister is impulsive."

London sighed hard, drawing his attention to her breasts. More than a handful there. He'd felt her softness as they danced, enjoyed their bodies moving together, and he knew that would translate well once he talked her into bed.

"Yes, she leaps before looking. She's lucky though because most things turn out for her. She doesn't make many missteps."

"Her marriage?"

19

"The worst mistake she's ever made. At least she's wised up and kicked her husband's arse out the door."

"Henry won't hurt her. He's a good man. You don't have to worry. He comes across as gruff, but he's a softy. You saw Geoffrey?"

She nodded, and Gerard decided Henry wouldn't mind him telling London the story if it reassured her about her sister's safety.

"Henry and I were staying with our other friend Sam and his wife Lisa, although she wasn't his wife at that stage. Someone was stalking Lisa. Sam has a farm near Christchurch, and when he couldn't be around, Henry and I stayed with Lisa and watched out for her. Geoffrey belonged to the elderly lady who lived next door to Lisa. The lady was the nosy type, and she was always at Lisa's house to borrow cups of sugar. Geoffrey used to come with her. He took an instant liking to Henry, although he growled at me, Lisa and Sam. The stalker escalated and killed Geoffrey's owner. The cops caught him the next day, in Lisa's house. After his owner's murder Geoffrey attached himself to Henry, and he's been with us ever since. Geoffrey's owner flirted with Henry too. Henry is kind to animals and old ladies. Your sister will be safe."

She smiled but her trepidation didn't lessen. His feline sensed her anxiety, and he glimpsed it in her blue eyes. He glanced at his watch.

"Storm in a Teacup is staying open late with so many people in town. Would you like to walk there for a late dessert and coffee? My friend's cousin owns the place...well, his wife. Lots of my friends will be there. I can introduce you to some of the people you'll be racing against tomorrow."

Her tense shoulders relaxed at his words.

"Emily makes a delicious chocolate brownie."

"I bake a good brownie."

"Ah," he said. "You have to come with me now so you can make a comparison."

"You had me at chocolate."

A laugh burst from him along with relief. London Allbright attracted him like no other woman, but she was timid. Or cautious. It made him wonder if it had been her and not her friend who had run into trouble with her drink in a pub.

"You'll like my friends. Most of them are married. If Saber and Leo are there, we'll quiz them about the course for the zombie run. I know there are obstacles—"

"Obstacles?" she blurted. "You never mentioned obstacles."

"Is that a problem?"

"No. Yes."

His brows rose, and he picked up his glass to drink the last of his beer.

"I'm not the most coordinated person when it comes to sports." She met his gaze and held it.

"Dancing is a sport." Yep, there was that zing again. Gerard wondered if he could persuade London to stay in Middlemarch.

She snorted. "Most people would dispute that statement."

"Not me." He reached for her hand, half expecting her to jerk from his touch. She surprised him, curling her fingers around his. This time he was ready for the zing, the satisfied purr of his feline. "Don't panic about the race or the obstacles. Henry and I entered for fun. The funds raised go to a good cause, and I will be with you every step of the way."

London finished her wine and stood, separating their hands. "Lead me to the chocolate. We didn't eat much dinner. I'm starving."

Gerard backed up to allow a newly arrived couple access to their table. "Let's go. I'll give you a tour of the town on the way to the café."

Outside, when he reached for her hand again, London let him weave their fingers together in a solid grip. Darkness had fallen, and a chill lingered in the air.

"Is your business in the town?"

"No, we purchased a lot on the outskirts of the town. We're building an office and storage facility, but at present we're operating out of a garage."

"You sleep in a garage?"

"No, the house is completed, but we're still working on the business setup."

London cast a sideways glance at him and he caught her, flashing her a charming smile. His signature smile, she was learning. A panty-wetting grin for sure. She'd bet women chased this man. His friend too, although Gerard hadn't paid attention to anyone except her while they'd been in the pub.

"The garage and petrol station," he said. "Post office, local school, the new sports grounds. The fields and changing sheds were the last community project. The school hall. That's where they hold the craft market, but on fine days, the stalls spill outside too."

London pictured the town with these events in full swing. It was quiet now, the streets devoid of traffic.

"Here's the café." He led her past several parked cars, through a gate and up three steps to an old-fashioned veranda. A pot of roses in full bloom perfumed the air. Gerard opened the door and gestured her inside.

Warmth and the scent of coffee welcomed her. A man gave a shout, and Gerard grinned, guiding her in the direction of a couple around Gerard's age.

"I thought we'd find you here," Gerard said and did a man-hug with the handsome dark-haired man.

"Beautiful Lisa," Gerard said, kissing the woman on the cheek.

"Behave. You know you'll make Sam crabby if you keep up that behavior," the woman said, after rolling her blue eyes skyward.

Gerard wrapped his arm around London's waist. "This is London Allbright. She and her sister are running with me and Henry tomorrow. London, this is my friend Sam and his wife Lisa. Sam, Henry and I were in the army together."

"Join us," Lisa said with a warm smile.

London liked her right away. "Jenny and Henry headed off for a walk, but Gerard lured me here with the promise of chocolate brownies."

"Smooth-talker," Lisa teased.

"I wanted to spend more time with London," Gerard confessed. "Brownies seemed a good bribe."

"It worked," London said.

He'd made her comfortable by bringing her here and introducing her to his friends. Royce had made her wary of men, hurt her with the way he'd made her small, then intensified her betrayal by taking off with Jenny. Because of Royce, their sisterly bond had frayed. Jenny's lack of belief in her when she'd tried to warn her had snapped the familial ties, and they'd only recently attempted to mend the broken trust. Jenny's accusations of jealousy still hurt, and anger at Royce for portraying her in this light and getting between her and her sister...

"Hey." Gerard leaned closer, and she breathed in his spicy scent. *Wow, almost better than chocolate.* "Where did you go?"

"Sorry, I didn't mean to zone out."

"I'll order," Gerard said. "What sort of coffee would you like?"

"A hot chocolate? I'll never sleep if I drink coffee now."

"Can't have that. I need you fighting fit for tomorrow."

"No point," Sam said with a wink at his wife. "Lisa and I have two fit teammates. We'll beat everyone."

London laughed along with Lisa at Gerard's derisive snort.

"Let's have a wager," Gerard said. "The slowest times out of our two teams buys the others lunch after the race."

"Done," Sam said and the two men shook hands to formalize the bet.

Good grief. London stared at Gerard. She'd thought he'd said this race was for fun and her lack of athleticism didn't matter. No pressure or anything.

Chapter 2

Zombies!

Middlemarch bed-and-breakfast

Despite her late night, London woke at seven. She stared around the unfamiliar room, her gaze alighting on the empty bed, twin to hers. Jenny truly hadn't come home last night, and London wasn't sure what to think. Henry seemed a decent man, but she'd thought Jenny might be wary and wouldn't jump into bed with any man who attracted her attention. Henry was not the first this trip and—no!

London stood. Who was she to judge her sister? She hadn't married Royce, hadn't gone through the agony of a disastrous relationship.

She flung off her T-shirt and sauntered to the en suite to flip on the shower. Luxury after staying in hostels. Jenny had wanted to stay in flash hotels but London refused to let her sister pay her entire way. Presenting London with the air tickets had been extravagant enough.

In the breakfast room, she ate a bowl of cereal and made herself a bacon sandwich, deciding she'd need the energy. She was drinking a second cup of coffee when Jenny rushed into the room from the entrance hall.

"Sorry I'm so late. I meant to be here in time for breakfast but one thing led to another and..." She threw up her hands with a laugh, her cheeks pink and her eyes sparkling with pure happiness. "I've showered, but I need to change into gear for the race. What are you wearing? What you have on now? I thought I'd wear shorts rather than leggings." She disappeared toward their room, only to bound back into the breakfast room. "I forgot to mention. Henry and Gerard are picking us up in half an hour. We have to enter and pay our fees then attend the official pre-talk where they go over the rules *yada, yada*." She vanished again, leaving London grinning.

This was the Jenny of old, so she'd stuff her judgey self away. If anyone deserved happiness, it was Jenny.

London drank the last of her coffee and stood. No shorts for her. She'd already donned leggings, a T-shirt and her sports shoes. Although she had no idea what she'd let herself in for, she was as ready as she could be.

Jenny rushed into the room, her hair dragged into a stubby ponytail and that happy smile intact. "Henry texted me. They're on their way."

"You like him, huh?"

"Yes. A lot. I was thinking I might extend my stay here."

"Oh, but I have to get back home or—"

"I know, sweetie. I know they said they'd keep a job for you, but is that job of yours worth it? There's no reason you can't get another. Competent secretaries and office assistants are in demand everywhere." Her smile widened as if she'd received a brain wave. "I mean, you like it here in New Zealand, and you enjoyed it in Melbourne during our stopover. What's stopping you from staying here and getting a job?"

"I don't have a work visa for a start," London said, reaching for practicalities. Jenny was the ideas person and didn't always face realities.

"Pooh! A minor thing. Think about it, London. Please? I want to stay. I like it over here, and it's not as if England has a hold on us now that Mummy and Daddy aren't alive. Promise me, you'll consider staying?"

Gerard appeared in the doorway. "Great. You're ready to go. Did you sleep well?"

London nodded. "I'll grab my purse. Won't be long."

"We'll meet you outside."

Jenny was waiting for her at the doorway, and they walked out together. "You'll consider staying longer?"

London shot a glance at her sister. Her jaw stuck out a fraction, as it did when she'd set her mind on achieving a goal. "Sure. I'll do that for you. Are you nervous? I am. What if I mess up the race? I've never done anything like this before."

"You'll be fine." She fluttered her eyelashes. "Henry is very strong. He'll help us over the obstacles."

Well. At least she'd got Jenny's mind off staying in New Zealand—for the moment. She refused to change her entire life to suit her sister's romantic leanings. Jenny had known Henry for one night, and London wasn't about to trust infatuation and lust over smart decisions.

London slid into the rear seat of the SUV with Gerard.

"You feeling bright-eyed and bushy-tailed?"

"If you mean fit and rested and ready to face zombies, I'll need another cup of coffee. I only had time for two."

Gerard laughed. "You need stronger stuff to deal with zombies. We should have hip flasks."

London grinned in return, her smile slipping a fraction when he reached for her hand. He squeezed her fingers. "Don't stress. Henry and I will help you as much as we can. We'd like to beat our friends, but it's not a big deal if we don't. I wanted to make sure you knew you should enjoy yourself. Did you bring your camera? We can leave our belongings in the vehicle during the race."

She lifted her gaze from their joined hands to his face. "Will I have time to take photos?"

"We'll make time before the race. Besides, Henry said he wanted to send some to his stepfather. He reckons he'll never believe we have a zombie invasion without proof."

"Stepfather?"

"Yeah, he's living in Perth, Australia, but Henry keeps asking him to come to Middlemarch and join us in the security business. Henry's mother remarried when he was five. His mother died when Henry was twelve and his stepfather brought him up. He's cool. We both want him to shift to Middlemarch and work with us."

London relaxed as Gerard chatted and held her hand. She liked him, his charm and easy-going nature. Sugar, she liked him enough that she was sitting quietly and not removing her hand from his grasp. The thought propelled her into motion and she pulled away from the physical contact.

"You keep touching me," she blurted.

His brows rose and his sensual lips quirked.

31

She mentally prodded herself and wrenched her gaze from his mouth. What the devil was wrong with her? She was thinking about kissing him, undressing him in her mind.

"I like you," he said, echoing her thoughts.

Damn man was a mind reader. She glanced out the window and recoiled when a zombie lurched toward their vehicle.

"Realistic, aren't they?" Gerard's voice sounded right next to her ear and his palm cupped her shoulder.

The man was touching her again. The contact slowed her speeding pulse, so she ignored him to gape at the group of sniggering zombies who'd witnessed her horrified start. They resembled the ones she'd seen on television. Pale faces with flesh hanging off...decomposing. Their hair hung in limp, greasy hanks and black and brown stains colored their mouths. Then, there was the blood.

London shuddered. "Now there's a good incentive to run fast."

Henry and Jenny stood beside Gerard, their bodies close and tucked into each other. His friend was a goner and Gerard couldn't blame him. Jenny was beautiful and bubbly and perfect for his more taciturn friend. Her sister, London, behaved with more caution. Sometimes, when he looked at her, he caught a faint wounded expression as if she harbored bad memories and they kept blindsiding her. She hovered around her sister in a protective mode, even though she was the younger one.

Sam and Lisa arrived and waved hello.

"How come you didn't team up with your friends?" London asked.

"They grew up here in Middlemarch and their friends asked if they wanted to be on their team before we moved to Middlemarch. Not that I'm worried. I think things have worked out for the best. We met you and Jenny."

London wrinkled her nose. "You are a flirt."

"Sometimes," he said. "But I'm not flirting with you. I want to get to know you better."

Her mouth fell open, and he tapped her chin.

"That's not a line."

"Jenny and I are leaving Middlemarch tomorrow."

"That's not what Jenny told Henry."

"I...she..." London trailed off with a frown.

Sid Blackburn, one of the Feline council, climbed onto a dais at the front of the crowd of runners and zombies and raised his hands for quiet. The excited chatter muted, and Sid welcomed everyone to the race.

"Now, the rules," Sid said. "Each member of your team has five red ribbons—one life for each kilometer of the race. Your goal is to get to the end of the race with as many ribbons as you can. The goal of the zombies is to deprive you of those ribbons and end your life. If you lose all your ribbons, you are dead and out of the race. Each of the ribbons you keep will contribute to your final score. The judges will combine your score with your time to determine your final placing. There are prizes for individuals and teams. Now, for the course," Sid continued. "Each competitor is required to complete the obstacles during the race. Five obstacles in total. We're keeping them a surprise." Sid chuckled, the sound rusty and full of amusement at the complaints fired from the audience. He held up his hands, still laughing.

"What else?" someone called.

"There are observers at each obstacle and each zombie territory. They are eagle-eyed and beyond bribery and will not hesitate to disqualify those who try to take shortcuts. The last thing—because we've had so many entries, we will start each four-person team at five-minute intervals. Questions?" Sid scanned the crowd. "Zombies, you have half an hour to get to your territories. We will start the competitors running at nine."

"When is our starting time?" London asked, drawing near to him when a quartet of zombies brushed too close.

Amusement filled him, but he didn't tease. Everyone had their phobias. "Ten twenty," he said.

Henry whispered something in Jenny's ear, and she giggled, standing on tiptoe to kiss him on the mouth.

"I'm nervous," London confessed. "I need a restroom."

"Come with me. I'll show you where they're located," Gerard said. "Just let me tell Henry where we're going."

He had to tap Henry on the shoulder twice before his friend pulled back from kissing Jenny. "Meet you at the start line. Ten past ten," he said, slicing minutes off their start time in case Henry got distracted. "Set the alarm on your watch. Don't be late."

"We'll be there," Henry said.

Gerard nodded, feeling more comfortable when his friend set his alarm. "Ready?" he asked London.

"Yes."

He took her hand and was happy when she didn't pull from the contact. The physical touch soothed his feline, made them both content. Weird, but he was letting instinct guide him in this new relationship.

Gerard and London wandered around the stalls that had sprung up since the previous night. A variety of things were on offer, ranging from food and drink to commemorative T-shirts and hats and zombie makeup.

"Sugar, the zombies come in different sizes," London muttered.

He turned in the direction she indicated and saw that the Feline council had organized a contest for the best zombie. Youngsters of all ages had dressed in ragged clothes and applied realistic blood and makeup.

London couldn't believe Gerard's patience with her pre-race. Her nerves stomped through the pit of her stomach like a platoon on the move and in a hurry to get to their destination. *Thump. Thump. Thump* right on her bladder.

The second time she said she needed to visit the restroom, he winked at her and said, "Nerves are good."

The clock ticked inexorably toward their start time, no matter how much her mind protested this race. Sports. Obstacles. Almost enough to send her fleeing to the restrooms again.

"It's time," Gerard said, and he tugged her hand. "We'll lock away our stuff in the vehicle now and go to the starting line."

Somehow, they'd walked around the stalls, taken zombie photos and passed their wait, holding hands. London wasn't sure why she didn't protest. Didn't understand it at all. The only thing that came to the forefront of her mind whenever she considered pulling from his grasp was that this felt right. She was comfortable with Gerard, and she was ruing her decision to sleep alone. If he signposted interest later today...

London turned her musings from that road and chose the upper path of caution and morals. Gerard might not express any interest once they finished this stupid race. He didn't believe she was as bad as she'd indicated. Yes, the next few hours held the makings of one of those clusty-f things people joked about.

"Are you sure it's race time?"

"Yes. Chin up." He grinned as she rolled her eyes. "That's my girl."

His words darted warmth to her heart and muted the worst of her nerves. She exhaled. "Let's do this."

The zombie race start line wasn't as crowded as she feared. Two elderly ladies had everyone under control, barking instructions and not putting up with tardy racers. They found Henry and Jenny and judging by the rash on Jenny's neck and her swollen kiss-marked mouth, they hadn't spent their wait running to and from the restroom or taking photos.

She turned to check Gerard's reaction to his friend and Jenny, her suspicions confirmed by his tetchy expression.

"I hope you and Jenny have enough energy left to escape zombies."

"We'll be fine," Henry said, his voice a low rumble.

"They retired early and slept late. I thought they'd spend the time recharging, not expelling more energy," Gerard whispered in her ear.

"Next," an elderly lady barked. Her glasses sparkled in the sun and not a fingerprint marred the surface. Her gray hair curled with precision and everything in her appearance screamed efficiency.

"Good morning, Valerie," Henry said.

The woman's nostrils flared and her expression pinched with disapproval. "You, my boy, are a wolf in sheep's clothing. You are a rogue."

Gerard barked out a laugh and Henry glared at his friend. Obviously, a private joke.

"Where are your zombie ribbons and your racing numbers?" she asked. "I need to check them and make sure they are on a belt and easily tugged free by any zombie who catches you." She counted each of their ribbons and supervised their placement. "Agnes will record your race numbers and tell you when you can start. Next!"

London shuffled forward with the others and listened to their hurried strategy session. Gerard had studied their course map while waiting for her and had mapped out the best route, which he communicated to Henry in short-form. She understood little of their discussion. The plan—they'd try to keep together, but there might be times where it would be better to split into pairs. She listened and took several deep, slow breaths. Her palms grew moist, and she wiped them on her leggings.

The next lady checked the placement of their numbers, wrote them on her chart, then lifted a timer to peer at the face. "Ten seconds to your start." She studied her timer. "Five, four, three, two, one, go!"

Henry, Jenny and Gerard bounded forward, London hesitating a fraction before forcing her legs to move. Too late to back out now. She had obstacles to conquer, zombies to escape.

"London," Jenny shouted.

Her sister's unspoken order prodded her into speed, and she ran, following the others along a grassy track. Spectators cheered as they passed. The other three waved. London was too busy breathing.

On the plus side, she was fitter than she had been since she'd done a lot of exercise this holiday. She kept running, taking in the green countryside and the stands of pine trees plus the weird piles of schist rock. Up ahead, she could see flickers of color—perhaps the group of runners who had left before them. Moans and groans and screams floated on the air, and she slowed.

"Zombies," Gerard said, jogging at her side.

"You look as if you're out for a Sunday stroll," she gasped out between pants.

His smile made her steps falter, and she tripped over a rut in the ground.

"Careful. I'm capable of carrying you if you sprain an ankle but it will be harder to escape zombies."

London splashed through a puddle, the cold water and mud clearing her fuzzy mind. "You couldn't carry me."

"Yes," he said. "I could. I'll prove it to you after the race."

The ground became even wetter, and London concentrated on her footing.

"First obstacle," Henry shouted over his shoulder. "Looks like tires."

Tires? What did that mean? London scanned the course ahead and saw two women running through the tires with a bouncy spring. Ah, she could do that. She gave silent thanks she'd packed a decent sports bra.

They ran faster down the slight incline and Henry bolted through the tires without hesitation, one foot placed in each before moving on to the next.

Jenny followed, then London.

Okay. Not too bad. London navigated the obstacle, taking care she followed the rules. She'd hate to get her team disqualified. Gerard followed her, and she tried not to imagine him watching her jiggling arse. It wasn't as if they'd ever see each other again after tomorrow.

She'd decided.

She was going home. Her sister could stay if she liked, but London didn't have the same financial security as Jenny. Besides, as much as she loved New Zealand, she'd need to go home and apply for a working visa from England. That wasn't something that could be done at the last minute.

"Good girl," Gerard said. "You okay?"

"Run out of puff," she gasped.

"Henry, you and Jenny go ahead. We'll walk for a few minutes."

"No, I can't—"

"No prob," Henry said. "Sounds as if we're almost at a zombie field, anyway. Meet you on the other side."

"Run," Jenny ordered.

London glared at her older sister. "I'm doing my best."

"You should exercise more."

Just to shut up Jenny, London took off at a trot. She hated this side of her sister, the bossy, competitive side. This event was a fun one, not life-or-death, and she'd be

41

having words with her sister later. She might have let Jenny back in her life, but she refused to take abuse in any form.

Now that she was following instructions, Jenny ran ahead to catch up with Henry.

"Does your sister always speak to you like that?"

"When she doesn't think I'm behaving in the proper manner. She means well."

"If you need to walk, that's what we'll do," Gerard said. "You warned us before we started that you weren't fit. I didn't care then, and it doesn't worry me now. The object is to join with the community and have fun."

"I do need to walk," she confessed.

Screams of laughter and loud moans drifted on the air and when they rounded a pile of schist, London spotted the first zombie field. Henry and Jenny darted through the zombies, passing other slower runners.

One zombie grabbed for a runner. The man feinted left and went right but the zombie anticipated him. His hand darted out, grasped a red ribbon and jerked it free. He let out a howl of triumph but the man didn't stop his dash toward the rest of the shambling zombies.

Gerard halted on the edge of the zombie territory. "Split up and run as fast as you can to the left. The zombies are smaller over that side. Don't worry if you lose a life. Keep running. Okay?"

"Yes."

"I'll give you four kisses for every life you have left at the end of the race," Gerard said.

She gaped at him. Was that a threat?

"That's a promise," he whispered with a wicked smile. "Go. Follow those runners, then split off. Meet you on the other side."

The group behind had caught them, but Gerard didn't seem worried. Jenny's shouts of horror speared London to action. She sprinted toward two zombies, one tall and skinny, the other chubby and covered with blood. Both sported red ribbons hanging from their belts.

At the last minute, she dodged to the left, instinct taking over. Her legs pumped. Her arms pumped. *Go. Go. Go.*

Mud splattered her calves. Cold water seeped into her shoes. The sun blazed overhead, determined to make her sweaty and plaster her hair to her head.

A zombie lined her up, and she zigzagged, then burst from the zombie territory, adrenaline keeping her speeding after the runners in front.

"Well done," Gerard said, his long strides catching him up. He slowed, keeping pace with her. "Still have all your lives. I lost one."

"That was fun."

"Told you."

"Hurry," Jenny shouted.

Henry said something to her, and she nodded, bounding off like a hare.

She, London decided, felt in charity with the tortoise. "What happens if we don't catch up with them?"

"It won't matter. As long as we finish, we get a time to combine with the others. Come on." He grasped her hand, and they ran together, his touch giving her new energy reserves.

The land undulated as they continued to run through and around more schist and into a stand of trees. Gerard released her hand and led the way through the trees.

Great view. London almost ran into a tree and ripped her gaze from Gerard's backside. A low-hanging scratchy branch whipped across her cheek and when she prodded the spot, her fingers came away with blood. Great. Jenny would never let her hear the end of that one.

On bursting through the trees they came to another obstacle. A huge web of rope pegged to the ground for the competitors to crawl beneath.

"Oh sugar," she muttered. "My butt is gonna get caught on that."

A chuckle beside her made London realize Gerard had heard her appalled whisper. He sidled up to her and patted her on the butt. "I like your shape. All of it."

London's mouth dropped open before a second bark of laughter had her pressing her lips together. Heat started at her cheeks and spread downward, frisking her breasts and settling at the juncture of her thighs. Sugar, this man had a smooth tongue.

"Truth," he said. "Should I go first?"

"Yes. Then I can form an opinion of your arse."

A flash of white showed his amusement. "Sounds fair." He plunged beneath the rope web and crawled at a steady pace that told her he'd done this many times.

"Go, London," Jenny shrieked, her voice holding approval and encouragement.

Ah, that reverse psychology stuff. Trust, Jenny.

London took a deep breath and followed Gerard. She wriggled and crawled, both boobs and butt giving her trouble. Finally, what seemed like a hundred hours later, she emerged through the gap at the other end.

"Good job." Gerard pressed a kiss to her lips. "Let's go."

Before she could register the kiss and decide what he meant by it, they were off again. Now she was breathless for a different reason.

The next field held more zombies, ranging in size from young to old. They shrieked and moaned and wobbled and shambled from side to side, in their search for food.

She spied Jenny ahead, laughing and zipping past two gray-haired zombies. One shook her fist in a very unzombielike gesture. Henry's rumble of amusement carried on the air.

"Go, go, go," Gerard encouraged her and she ran into their territory. She darted left. She darted right. She ran straight ahead. Hands grasped. Hands tugged at her ribbons. One pulled free.

She kept running and almost lost another ribbon, her quick feint to the left saving her.

Once she sprinted over the boundary line, she kept running, knowing Gerard would catch her. She glimpsed Henry and Jenny before they disappeared around a corner.

London huffed and puffed around the same corner and came to an appalled halt.

"Why are you stopping?"

"I'm not good with climbing stuff."

"No different than climbing a tree," Gerard said.

"I don't do trees. I've never climbed trees." She watched Henry give Jenny a boost up the rope webbing attached to the wall. Her sister crawled up the wall with ease. For an instant, she rested on the top of the wall, then disappeared over the other side.

"Keep running," Henry shouted to her sister. "I'll catch up."

He sounded as if he was having fun.

"I'll give you a boost and Henry will help you over the top." Gerard grabbed her before she could argue. She let out a girlie shriek, instinct making her grab for the webbing.

"Do you need another shove?"

"No. Let me catch my breath."

"Are you sure? I'd love a good reason to grope your butt."

"Stop flirting with her," Henry groused, although London was close enough to see the quirk of his lips. He stretched out his arm and offered his hand. "Grab my hand and I'll pull you to the top."

London doubted he'd be strong enough to pull her up, but her legs were so shaky they weren't propelling her upward. She reached up and an instant later, he'd hauled her up and she perched on top of the wall. Then she made the mistake of looking down.

Chapter 3

Shocking Disruption

Gerard grinned up at Henry and received a wink in return. "Go! I'll be with you in a moment, English."

"I hate this rope stuff and the way it moves." Her prim accent held a touch of fear.

"It's not far," Henry said, his tone soothing. "There is a soft landing pad, so no one gets hurt. Close your eyes and go at your own pace. Gerard will come to help you."

Gerard gave his friend a curt nod, and Henry jumped from the top. The air whooshed from the landing pad as Henry's bulk hit. London whimpered, and Gerard climbed the webbing, arms and legs pulling, pushing. In ten seconds he reached the top and discovered London descending at the pace of a sick snail. He slid his legs over the top and maneuvered to her side. The webbing swung with his weight and she moaned, her limbs trembling.

"London, do you trust me?"

She trembled.

"London." He spoke sternly to pierce her panic. "Do you trust me?"

She gave a jerky nod.

Pleasure suffused him at her response. *Not the time.* "Good." And he turned her head to kiss her, really kiss her as he'd been longing to since he first spied her across the pub. The second she relaxed, he threw himself backward, wrenching her off the webbing.

She screamed against his mouth, but he didn't release his grip. Curvy. Perfect. He couldn't wait to investigate more of her luscious body. An instant later, he hit the landing pad, and grunted when London's flailing hand almost gelded him.

"That will teach you," Benjamin Urquart, one of the Feline council commented. The slight-built man wrinkled his pixie nose while his piercing green gaze brimmed with silent laughter and approval. "You have both completed this obstacle. You'd better get up before the next competitors arrive."

"Stop moving, English," Gerard whispered. "We're safe and alive, but if you keep thrashing around, I won't be able to perform once you succumb to my charm."

"That might work with other women but it won't with me," she snapped as she rolled clear.

"I'd believe you if you hadn't kissed me back."

"I-I never!" An intense wave of pink bloomed in her cheeks.

"Yeah, English. You did. We will share a bed, eventually."

Her mouth dropped open, and he stood, offering a hand to help her up. She accepted his aid and once they were both upright, he started running. "Come on. Henry and Jenny expect us to put in a good time. We can discuss this later."

"You are impossible."

"I'm charming and sexy, and I want to share my good traits with you."

"Good traits?" She snorted but broke into a run at his side.

"Sounds as if there is another zombie territory up ahead."

They ran past two mature pine trees, the sharp scent of the foliage clearing his lust. One kiss hadn't put a dent in his craving for her. He was feeling a sneaking sympathy for his friend Sam, who had waited for years to claim his mate. Gerard's human mind hadn't accepted this soul mate thing but his feline was leading him around by the dick. His feline side wanted London Allbright with her cool English accent, rounded curves, fear of heights and indifference to sports. Not the woman he'd pictured but the instant he touched her nothing else seemed to matter.

"Not another hill. My legs are wobbling like a strawberry jelly."

"You're doing great." The truth. She was trying and keeping whining to a minimum. "Have I told you I'm great with massage?"

"Yes." She started up the slope, the moans and shouts from the zombie field becoming louder. "Where did you learn massage again?"

"One of my girlfriends worked in sports medicine, and she taught me the correct way to massage."

"How many girlfriends have you had?"

Gerard considered the question and gave up counting once he reached ten. Those were the more serious ones that had lasted at least two weeks and longer. He didn't count the casual pickups or one-night stands. What guy hadn't had those? "A few."

"Over five?"

"Eight," he said, picking his favorite number. "I'm older than you."

"I'm twenty-three. Twenty-four next month."

"Twenty-nine," Gerard said. "So it stands to reason I'd have more relationships."

They crested the hill and halted to stare at the flat clearing below. Grassy with a stream running through, which split the area along the quarter mark. The zombies had trampled the grass and the stony ground near the banks of the stream appeared muddy. A plan formed.

"We should run through the stream. The other runners are going through the larger portion and the zombies are picking them off. We can take them by surprise if we slog through the water. It's not deep."

"How do you know?"

"It's ankle depth and, at worse, cold. We'll need to take care on rocks but once we're past the zombies then we can run along the bank."

"Couldn't we creep through the trees around the clearing?"

"They're roped off. Can you see the red barrier on each side?"

"Now you've told me. You have good eyesight."

"There will be a scrutineer making sure we navigate the clearing. Come on. I can see Henry."

"Jenny?"

Gerard scanned the runners and spotted her number as she dodged a big zombie. "Yeah, she just lost a life. Let's go. Clear on the plan?"

"Yes. I will get wet and muddy."

Gerard chuckled at her forlorn tone. "I hear they have photographers at the finish line."

"Say it isn't so," she muttered as she followed him.

She tripped and fell into him, almost knocking him off his feet. The proximity, her scent beneath the mud and the hint of blood from the scratch on her cheek drove him crazy. He held her until she regained her balance then a fraction longer to soothe his feline. "Okay?" His voice emerged rough and raw, the sound pushed past his protruding canines. Bloody hell. Sam had informed him of the loss of control, and Sam's cousins, Felix and Leo, had backed him up, yet Gerard hadn't believed them, not a word.

"Sorry. My feet didn't go the way my brain told them to."

As the path widened, he grasped her hand, his feline appreciating the physical contact while it kept his English lady from falling. His feline genes gifted him with a good sense of balance and surefootedness. "Faster," he said, increasing his pace.

"There are more zombies here."

"Don't worry. We'll get past them." He scanned the clearing and noted a zombie climbing over the red tape and rejoining the pack. Blood coated his white shirt and faded jeans while his hair lay in dusty dreads against his head. Whoever had done the makeup had done a brilliant job. These zombies looked like the real deal.

"Through this entrance," the scrutineer ordered, straightening from his lean against the trunk of a tree.

Gerard yanked London through and sprinted for the stream, dragging her behind him. The water came to knee height, and it was bloody freezing. London moaned as the frigid water seeped through her leggings.

"Come on, English. We need to move before they come after us."

A whistle blew without warning. "You!" the scrutineer hollered. "You're going out of bounds."

Then a mournful howl filled the air, raising the small hairs at his scruff. Gerard's head snapped around to search for Henry. "Fuck. That doesn't sound good."

London tensed, the howl containing so much pain that tears sprang to her eyes. A second howl followed before the echoes of the first died.

"Come on," Gerard shouted and dragged her from the stream.

He plunged through the mass of zombies, clearing a path with his determined bulk and sharp curses. Most of the zombies were staring in the direction of the howl, which was coming from the trees.

"What is it? What's going on?" London demanded.

"Henry needs us," Gerard snapped. "Faster."

The zombies recovered from their trance and hands grabbed at their ribbons.

Another howl, louder and full of anguish, echoed through the clearing, and Gerard tossed zombies out of his way.

When she couldn't keep up, he dragged her with determination and she lost her footing.

"Get the fuck out of my way." Gerard growled and the circle of zombies took a collective step back.

With their way clear, Gerard yanked her to the red tape surrounding the clearing. He stepped over, forging a path in the long grass. The howls were softer now, and it was easier to pinpoint their location.

London dug in her heels, not sure she wanted to approach this creature—whatever it was. It sounded in so much agony.

"London." Gerard's tone held demand, and she obeyed before she stopped again.

Another howl rang out and Gerard released her hand with a curse, plunging through the tangle of undergrowth.

"Henry."

London frowned. He'd mentioned Henry before, but he wouldn't make this hair-raising noise. Goose bumps formed on her arms and legs, and she glanced over her shoulder, scanning the gnarled trunks of the trees, the profusion of green ferns and the dead leaves underfoot. It was darker under the trees. Creepy.

"Fuck," Gerard said, and it was the shock in his voice that got her feet moving again in his direction.

"What is it?"

"Stay there, London."

Something in the way he said her name instead of his teasing *English* made her disobey. Something was wrong, and she—

London gasped and rushed forward.

Jenny lay on the ground, a knife protruding from her chest and bright red blood covering her pale blue T-shirt.

Gerard grabbed London before she could get to her sister. "No," he ordered, his tone sharp. "We can't help her now." His tone gentled. "We'll call the cops and they will help her."

Tears blurred her vision, and even though her heart railed against his instructions, her mind forced her to accept the truth. She and Jenny would never have another argument because someone had stabbed her sister in the chest. Someone had murdered Jenny.

Isabella Mitchell appeared behind them. "What is it? What's wrong? I smell blood."

Gerard glanced at Henry, saw the glassy-eyed shock on his friend's face as he knelt by Jenny, then looked past a pale London to Isabella. "Do you have a phone?"

"Yeah." Blonde Isabella, Leo Mitchell's mate, pulled a satellite phone from her jacket.

"You'd better call the cops." He shifted aside a fraction so she could see Jenny Weaver and the knife protruding from her chest.

She nodded and made the call.

Gerard appreciated a calm woman who didn't rattle easy. He turned to London. "Stay right there, London. We don't want to destroy the scene."

"Is-is she d-dead?"

"I'm sorry, English."

Henry lifted his head and another one of those eerie howls filled the air. *Crap.* Too many humans around for Henry to lose control.

Isabella edged closer, taking care where she stepped. "Saber and Leo are on their way. They'll take care of Henry," she said. "Did he do it?"

"No," Gerard snapped, glancing at his friend again. "They'd only just met, but he was halfway in love with her." Henry didn't react to his words, which worried Gerard. He'd never seen Henry act like this, not even after the bad times they'd faced together in the army.

"Who is this?" Isabella jerked her chin in London's direction.

"London Allbright," London said in a tight voice.

Gerard heard the tight-held emotion in her, the hovering tears and wanted to hold her. He couldn't though, not when Henry needed him.

"Isabella?"

Gerard recognized Saber Mitchell's voice. Part of the Feline council, he was also the oldest Mitchell brother. Gerard knew he'd do right by Henry, not that Gerard intended to walk away from his best friend.

Saber and Leo, Isabella's mate, came to a halt by Isabella.

"Fuck," Leo said in vast understatement.

"The cops are on the way," Isabella said. "They're coming from the station, so it will take them at least fifteen minutes."

"Good," Saber said. "That will give us time to check the scene. Isabella, you're best at this."

She nodded and approached the body.

Gerard heard a whimper and turned his head. He watched London's face crumple. Tears rolled down her face as she stared at Jenny, at the brown hilt of the knife protruding from her chest. The pool of blood that had settled beside her sister. On shaky feet, she edged closer.

"Leo," Isabella said in a sharp tone.

Leo grabbed London before she could get to her sister. He whispered to her, and Gerard couldn't hear what he said, but London cried in earnest and Leo wrapped her in a soothing embrace. Gerard shot a glance at Isabella and saw she didn't appreciate Leo touching another woman. The feeling was mutual. If it wasn't for Henry, Gerard would have pushed between the pair and taken London in his arms.

"Henry." Gerard tugged at his arm. "What happened? Henry!" Gerard stood and wrenched on Henry's arm.

His friend gave an anguished howl, and Gerard heard London's gasp. Crap. Henry needed to get control of himself before the cops arrived. None of them could help Jenny if Henry scared the cops, and they panicked. He slapped Henry over the face. It had the opposite effect.

59

Henry shifted farther into his wolf, his features becoming sharper and more canine.

"The cops are here already." Isabella's voice carried. "No, it's just Hannah. He hasn't called in cops from Dunedin to help."

"Idiot," Saber muttered. "I'll meet him. Get Henry under control."

Gerard didn't need the warning. He leaned closer to Henry and spoke in a harsh, clipped voice. "Soldier, I need you to get hold of yourself. Attention!"

Henry's entire body jerked. His shoulders straightened, and he climbed to his feet. His big friend trembled, his brown eyes glassy with shock.

"We'll find who did this, Henry. I promise," Gerard whispered. "I promise."

The local cop was nearing retirement, and his mind wasn't on the job these days. According to local gossip gathered since he and Henry arrived in Middlemarch, finding two bodies had been the final straw. PC Tom Hannah scowled at the third body, then huffed as he pulled up his trousers and settled them into position on his well-padded hips.

"Who found her?" the policeman asked.

"Henry," Saber said.

Hannah surveyed Henry and scowled again.

60

"This is my fault," Henry whispered, loud enough for Hannah to hear and jump to conclusions.

"I have backup coming. I want you to return to the clearing," Hannah ordered. "You've trampled the scene enough. Go!" He threw up his hands. "I don't know what is wrong with the people around here."

Gerard looked to Saber, and he gave a curt nod.

"We'll take London," Isabella said. "You get Henry."

Gerard took Henry's arm. "Come on, mate. Let's move and let the cops take care of Jenny."

When Henry didn't budge, Gerard exerted pressure around his shoulders. Hell, his friend was going the stubborn route.

"This is all my fault," he repeated.

"How? You didn't do it." Aware of the cop's ears flapping, Gerard stopped asking questions. "Henry." He forced an order into his tone, and to his relief, Henry allowed Gerard to lead him into the zombie clearing.

They joined Saber and the others. More runners kept coming and Gerard saw that Leo and the scrutineer were directing the arriving competitors around the clearing toward the next obstacle. He scanned the zombies and runners still present.

"I saw a zombie come out of the trees as London and I entered the zombie territory. I thought he'd gone to relieve himself."

Saber's look was sharp. "Recognize him?"

"He looked like a zombie." Gerard scowled, trying to remember. "Hell, it could have been a female. He or she was big."

"See them in the crowd?"

Gerard studied the loitering zombies. They chatted to one another and sipped from water bottles, their faces garish with makeup. Their grins displayed blackened teeth. One had bloody teeth. They kept moving, shifting positions within the knots of groups, and with their costumes and makeup, none of them stood out as individuals. The guy he'd seen had been tall. Most of these zombies were shorter, teenagers and kids. He had seen no one leave, but maybe one of the other zombies had noticed.

"I can't see the zombie, but they are similar. We could question the zombies and ask how many were here." Gerard wanted to go to London, but stayed put. He'd met London last night. His feline wanted her. He was sure she was the one for him, but Henry needed him more. If he were in the same position, Henry wouldn't hesitate to offer his help—whether he asked for it or not—and he could do nothing less.

"The other cops might not be here for half an hour or longer," Saber said. "Henry." His tone was stern alpha leader, and Henry's shoulders straightened from their slump. "Did you do this?"

"No." Henry's voice was gruff, his eyes narrowed at the accusation. "She was my mate. I wanted to keep her."

"Did you argue about it? Her staying?" Saber demanded.

"No, she wanted to stay in Middlemarch. I told her she could live with me if she wanted, but she said she'd rent a house. She was just out of a bad marriage, and she wanted to take things slow. I was fine with that. I knew my mind." The grief in his words made Gerard's throat tighten. He'd never seen Henry like this over a woman.

"Why was she in the bush?" Gerard asked.

"I don't know for sure. A toilet break? One minute she was with me, and the next she disappeared. There was so much noise. I didn't see where she went. I dodged the zombies and caught her scent. And then, I found her."

"Did you see anyone?" Saber demanded.

Gerard frowned. "Get a whiff of a foreign scent?" He had detected nothing out of the ordinary, but then he hadn't thought to check for other scents. There was the blood and greenery, a hint of mud and water. "Footprints? Hell, we tromped through there to get to Henry." He answered his own question. "Anyone else notice anything?"

"Just the blood," Saber said. "Leo and Isabella mentioned nothing unusual."

"We need to split up, question the zombies and the competitors who are still here," Gerard said. "Before the rest of the cops get here."

"Agreed. I recognize a few of the runners. I'll start with them," Saber said. "Henry, you'd better not ask questions. The cops will want to talk to you."

"I want to inspect the zombies. I'll keep Henry with me." Gerard glanced at Henry. "Stay with me and say nothing."

"I want to stay with Jenny." Emotion gripped him, made his voice hoarse.

"Not now, buddy. Soon, okay?" Gerard urged Henry to move. "This is important. We need to do this before the cops arrive." When Henry remained rooted to the spot, Gerard grasped his forearm and tugged hard. "Henry, do you want to help Jenny or not?"

"What about London? You should be with her. She needs you."

Trust Henry. He'd always been able to read him. "London thinks you murdered her sister. I want both of you in my life and right now, I need to help you. Isabella and Leo are looking after London."

Thoughts of London made his mind drift. A glimpse of several men in police uniform arriving in the clearing helped him to focus. "Crap, the cops are here faster than I thought."

Chapter 4

Investigation

London stood with Isabella and Leo Mitchell, her mind stunned and sluggish. Jenny was gone, and their last interaction had been Jenny sniping at her, making London feel lacking. Even though, in her heart, London knew Jenny had goaded her on purpose to boost her determination to beat the obstacle, a sliver of hurt remained. A remnant of their shared past. The notion ran through her mind as fast as a racing greyhound. Round and round. Round and round. Round and round.

Jenny.

Dead.

It hardly seemed fair.

After the years of her horrid marriage and the estrangement between them, the harsh words, they'd made up and celebrated with a trip down under.

They'd almost been sisters again, and now Jenny...someone had killed her.

Her fists clenched at her side and her weight shifted. She needed to do something, but what?

"Stay here," Isabella said in a low undertone. "The Middlemarch cop can't organize himself out of a paper bag, but we have to let him go through the motions. We will find who did this to your sister. I promise you that." The blonde woman grasped her upper arms and shook her.

Maybe it was to make sure London was paying attention. These people were strange. What could they do that the police couldn't? Her thoughts shifted to Henry. All that blood. She shuddered at the memory, the peculiar aroma of fresh blood. Bile rose up her throat, and she wrenched from Isabella's grasp. She ran toward the nearby undergrowth and vomited.

With her stomach empty and her throat burning, she straightened and wiped the back of her hand over her mouth.

"Here," Isabella said, thrusting out her hand. "You want gum?"

London hesitated before deciding the gum trumped her gross breath, even if she threw up again.

Her thoughts returned to Henry. His face...she was sure she'd seen... No. Her mind was playing tricks on her.

"Something's happening," Leo said in a low voice.

The cops grouped together in a discussion. PC Hannah pointed at Henry. Two cops broke away from the group and headed toward Henry and Gerard.

"Idiots," Leo muttered. "Anyone with half a brain would know he didn't do this. He was halfway in love with the girl. They were m—"

Isabella jerked her head in London's direction and Leo broke off.

"Who did it then?" London burst out. "Henry was the only one with her."

"Henry spent last night and all the morning with your sister. Don't you think if he'd had sinister designs on her he'd have killed her in a less public place? He's a big man. He had plenty of opportunity to have his wicked way then dispose of the body. What you're implying isn't logical." Isabella's flat, concise explanation tore holes through her conviction.

London thought back. Jenny had liked Henry too. While she'd picked up guys in places they'd stayed, she'd always been happy to leave the next morning and she'd always returned to her room. That hadn't happened with Henry.

Henry had been different, an exception.

Henry had...

London felt her brows squeeze together in a frown. Henry's face...it hadn't been her imagination. For an instant he'd appeared...animalistic. Yes, that was the word.

"How can you promise to catch the p-person who did this to Jenny?" London sucked in a breath to grasp at control because she could hear the hysterical note in her voice. "I—" Her voice cracked, and she inhaled, swallowed. "What can you do?"

Isabella and Leo exchanged a speaking glance, although not one in a language she understood. Was it her imagination or were there weird undercurrents here?

"No! I didn't do it!"

London whirled around to see two cops yanking on Henry's beefy arms. Henry pulled away and one cop fell.

Gerard helped up the policeman and said something to Henry.

"Come on," Isabella said. "We need to hear this, listen to the charges." She took off with long strides and her husband flanked her. London scurried to catch up. This was Jenny. If Henry had murdered her sister, she wanted to know why.

"Henry. Go with them," Gerard said in a sharp voice, taking hold of Henry's free arm. "Don't make trouble. We will fix this. Get you a lawyer. I promise we will fix this." He spoke in an undertone, for Henry's ears only.

"You can't bring Jenny back." Stark emotion shimmered in Henry, his brown eyes glassy with the sheen of unshed tears.

"We can find who did this," Gerard said. "That will be a start for you and London."

"London. Fuck, is London all right?"

And Henry returned, his brain jolted into gear again.

"London is upset. I'll look after her." His lips twisted as he forced a grin at his friend. "You're not the only one hung up on an English lady."

"You too?"

Gerard nodded, glad the cops had let him speak to Henry. Most cops would have pulled out their Taser and fired without another warning. Henry's size had worked for him. Neither of the cops were big and having to drag Henry to where they'd left their cars made them cautious.

"Ready?" one cop asked, his tone skirting sarcastic.

Henry nodded and let them lead him away.

"They arrested him?" Isabella asked.

"Read him his rights," Saber answered, a trace of disgust in his gaze. "Hannah's retirement can't come soon enough. We need cops who will use their brains. Someone younger."

"Preaching to the choir, bro," Leo said.

"What's the plan?" Isabella asked. "No one I've spoken to saw anything. They were too busy trying to avoid zombies."

"Same with the zombies," Gerard said. "And there is no one the size of the guy I saw as London and I entered the clearing."

"What guy?" London asked.

"I saw a zombie come from the bush, not far from where we found Jenny. He was big—at least I'm assuming it was a man—but most of these zombies are teenagers and kids. There are several big teenagers, but I'm certain I saw an adult. The zombies I questioned denied taking a toilet break in the bush."

"Have you told the policemen you saw someone?" London demanded. "It wasn't Henry?"

Gerard bit his tongue, counseling himself to patience. She didn't know Henry like he did. "They wore a zombie costume." He'd said it was a zombie.

"Just double-checking." Bright pink collected in her cheeks and she averted her gaze.

"Cops are coming," Saber said in an undertone. "Can we go, officers? I'm the organizer of the race and they're expecting me at the finish line."

"You can go after we take your names and ask you questions."

They questioned Saber first, and he left after telling them he'd arrange representation for Henry.

It was three hours later before the cops allowed the rest of them to leave. A forensic team arrived and was still hard at work when they left.

"London, come on. We can't help Jenny here." Gerard slid his arm around her waist. She jerked away and his arm slipped to his side.

"I-I—"

"I'd never hurt you. Henry didn't do this, London. I don't know who murdered your sister, but it wasn't him or any of my friends."

London didn't truly believe Henry murdered her sister. Not now that her brain had worked through everything she knew using rational thought. She'd seen them together, noticed Henry's gentleness with Jenny. They'd made love before the race. That much had been obvious to her at the starting line. Jenny had been happy, happier than London had ever seen her. Henry had seemed equally smitten.

"I'm sorry. I'm a bit jumpy."

"Understandable. Let's clean up, get into warmer clothes. We'll make a plan. You can stay with me."

"No," London said. "I'll book in at the bed-and-breakfast for the rest of the week or at least as long as I'm needed here. I need to rearrange my flights, notify our friends."

"Your parents?"

"Both died when we were in our late teens. There is no one else."

"Jenny's ex?"

"No! We have nothing to do with Royce. He-Jenny—no!"

"If you change your mind, you're welcome to stay with me. We have a spare bedroom. I don't expect you to share my bed."

London's heart stuttered like a motorboat engine unwilling to start. She inhaled and her pulse jolted to something resembling normal speed. Then shame filled her. She shouldn't be thinking of sex when her sister lay dead. She managed a nod and forced her legs to move. Her muscles ached from running and climbing and crawling. The mud had dried on her skin and it itched. She couldn't wait to wash away the day. She wished she could scour away the truth with the same ease.

Gerard and Henry's property, outskirts Middlemarch

"If this zombie that Gerard saw is responsible for the murder, I don't understand why none of us sensed his presence," Isabella said.

"There was so much blood plus the weird stuff the zombies sprayed over themselves as part of their costumes. I tried not to decipher the scents," Saber said.

"Same with me." Gerard paced around the kitchen table where Sam, Lisa and Sam's cousins had congregated to decide on a plan of attack.

Sam tipped his chair, balancing it on two legs. "We need to question the other zombies again. You guys said you weren't able to get to all of them before the cops started their questioning. We have their names and most of them are locals. Who was the scrutineer? We need to check with the makeup girls. They might remember a big guy. They did the makeup."

"We need to do a background check on Jenny and London," Isabella said. "It makes little sense that someone would randomly pick Jenny and stab her. This smacks of something else. Love gone wrong or revenge."

Gerard nodded. "The cops think so too. They didn't hesitate to arrest Henry. I know there was an ex-husband." He frowned, replaying their conversations. "London lives in Bath and Jenny lives in London. The city," he added when Sam grinned.

"Anything else?" Isabella asked. "I have contacts, but the more information we give them the better."

"London works as a secretary." Gerard wrinkled his brow. "Can't remember what Jenny does. Henry will know."

"You should talk to Henry before you speak to your contact." Lisa reached over to squeeze Gerard's hand. "This might take time but we'll get Henry out of jail."

"I'd feel better if Hannah wasn't in charge," Saber said.

"Hopefully someone more senior takes over the investigation," Isabella offered. "First, Hannah isn't competent and second, he's lazy. He'll pass off the responsibility if he can. Gerard, we'll try to get in to see Henry. If they won't let us, we'll ask his lawyer to get the details for you."

"I'll speak with London. Wait...there was something else. When we were in the pub last night London froze. She thought she saw someone she knew. When I asked her she brushed it off, but I felt her panic."

Isabella nodded. "You need to ask her again. It might be something that will help us."

"I dropped her off at the bed-and-breakfast. I'll give her an hour then call her and ask her out to dinner. Is Storm in a Teacup open late tonight?"

"Yes," Saber said. "Emily wanted to capitalize on the extra people in town. I'll call her and book you a table. About seven?"

"Yes, that will work," Gerard said. "God, I hate this. They were so quick to charge Henry. Henry doesn't do well in confined spaces."

"Is he moon-called?" Saber demanded.

"Only if he doesn't shift on a regular basis," Gerard said in a grim voice. He'd considered this, but they'd get Henry out of custody before the full moon. "Since we've lived in Middlemarch we've run most days. It's part of why we based our business here. If he goes for the next week without shifting, his body will force a shift on him once the moon is full."

"Crap. When is full moon?" Isabella asked.

"Seven, no eight days." Gerard calculated in his head. Easy these days since he lived with a werewolf. "Do you think we can get him out on bail?"

"Not for a murder charge." Sam's voice was grim. "They'll say he's a danger to others."

"We'll get the lawyer to work on bail and to learn the details of the charges," Saber said. "If we run into problems, we might have to break him out."

Saber wasn't joking and the grim reality slapped them all. Jail was the least of Henry's problems. If he turned wolfish, the government agencies would line up to take custody of Henry. His friend would never be free.

London ignored the peal of her cell phone in the other room. Instead, she continued her shower. No matter how much she increased the hot water, she couldn't get warm. Using Jenny's laptop, she'd done an internet search on arriving back at the bed-and-breakfast. Then, following the instructions she'd found, she'd rung the British High Commission in Wellington to inform them of Jenny's death.

They'd told her they'd locate Royce and inform him. The man she'd spoken to had been helpful and explained that since the manner of death was suspicious, an autopsy would take place. After this, which might take time, they'd release her body. London could then repatriate Jenny home to England or have her buried in New Zealand.

He'd referred her to a website for further details and told her how to register the death online. She'd scribbled notes, her tears blurring her sight and making the ink swirl on the page. He'd been blunt, yet helpful too, and told her to call again if she had questions.

She swirled her fingers over her arm and the bubbles created by the shower gel and held up her right hand to stare at her wrinkly skin. Her chest and throat throbbed with tightness. She kept swallowing and swallowing. Nothing eased the pressure.

With Jenny gone, she felt so alone. Truly alone and indecisive.

She'd been so happy at her and Jenny's reconciliation and had let her sister plan the trip, London's one stipulation that she pay for her own accommodation and meals. Backpacker accommodation had been a novelty for Jenny and she'd enjoyed the people they'd met, fellow tourists. Now, London wasn't sure what to do. Of course, she'd stay for a short time, but eventually she had to go home.

Jenny had wanted to stay. She'd trusted Henry, and the more London thought of the relationship the more she doubted her initial reaction. Henry hadn't acted guilty or in any way suspicious. He'd been distraught.

His friends believed him innocent, and if that was the way she leaned too, that meant Jenny's real killer still roamed free. Perhaps they'd left Middlemarch already.

Why? Her mind kept circling the motive. Everyone liked Jenny. Oh, she could be judgmental and impatient and a plain bitch. London knew her sister's weaknesses as well as she knew her own. But none of that had been present during their holiday. For the first time in ages, Jenny had returned to her normal self, her happiness bubbling over and spreading to everyone they met with an infectious joy.

Her phone rang again. London frowned, wondering who could be calling her. Her friends knew she was away on holiday, and she hadn't given her number out to many—

Gerard?

London stepped out of the shower and dried off with a towel. On unfastening her hair from the knot she'd secured it in to keep dry, she scowled at the scratches on her cheek. She'd looked better. Once dressed in dry jeans, a thick sweater and wooly socks, she checked her phone. It was Gerard.

She hesitated, then hit redial.

"London." Gerard's deep voice sent a quiver through her. "Are you all right?"

Not really. "I'm fine. Just had a shower to warm up."

"I wondered if you'd have dinner with me. You shouldn't be alone."

"No, it's..." She trailed off, uneasy at his words. "Why?"

"The cops might think they have their guy, but they haven't. He's wandering loose, maybe in Middlemarch. We don't know what he's thinking. I'd feel better if you weren't alone."

And now she was cold again because his words echoed her thoughts. But she hadn't thought, hadn't considered danger for herself. "Thank you. I'd enjoy the company."

"I'll pick you up at six thirty and we'll go to Storm in a Teacup or we could go to the pub."

"Storm in a Teacup sounds nice." She'd enjoyed their visit the previous night and maybe someone to talk with would help dispel the numbness in her mind. "Six thirty," she agreed.

Alone in the room, she went through Jenny's belongings, since she'd have to move out soon. Jenny's clothes and possessions. Packing brought tears to her eyes since each garment held a wealth of memories. The sparkly red shirt Jenny had purchased in Melbourne and the skinny jeans London had eyed with envy because she'd never cram her chunky legs into the tight denim. A possum-and-merino hat and scarf set she'd purchased in Queenstown. London stroked the scarf and tears filled her eyes. It was cooler today. She'd coveted the hats and scarves in the shop but couldn't afford to buy one, not if she'd wanted to eat and visit attractions during the rest of their holiday. She'd told Jenny she had plenty of hats and scarves at home. The truth, yet not.

She set them aside to wear, telling herself Jenny wouldn't mind.

Home. Royce? *Sugar*. Should she call Royce?

Officially, he was still Jenny's husband. The man in Wellington had said they'd contact Royce, but should she too, for decency's sake? She'd mentioned Jenny and Royce's separation and the restraining order against him to the cops. She hadn't told the rotund policeman, for a crazy instant, she'd thought she'd seen Royce last night.

A ludicrous idea.

Planes and Royce didn't mix as he hated flying. One of the many reasons Jenny had decided on a trip to the other side of the world.

Reassured by the thought, she kept on with her folding and going through Jenny's things. She pulled out Jenny's suitcase and noticed something tucked into an inner pocket. Papers. Probably a hard copy of their travel itinerary. Jenny had copies on her laptop and phone and this was a backup. She pulled out the sheath of papers and flicked through them before coming to an envelope with her name written on it in her sister's writing.

She stared at the papers, the words jumbling as more tears fell. Then, long seconds later, she opened the envelope and started reading.

Chapter 5

Creepy Feeling

Gilcrest Station

The man stomped across the open ground, fury still pumping through his veins hours after the deed. The bitch had taunted him, told him she had a new lover, a new life, and she didn't need him any longer. Surplus to requirements, she'd said. Surplus!

He strode along the path bordering a river. Several fishermen hailed him as he passed, their friendly greetings grating on his nerves. Bah! Why were they so happy? Stuck in this back end of the world with no entertainment, no decent restaurants, no whisky. God, he'd had to resort to common stuff when he only drank premium Scottish.

Why had the woman traveled halfway across the world? She'd pushed him to act.

It was her fault she was dead.

He stopped at a bend in the river and dropped onto a seat placed beneath a willow. The afternoon had turned nippy, the cold whistling over the piles of schist rock and striking his face.

He cursed and cursed again.

All his problems started with women.

If she hadn't taunted him, hadn't boasted of her new love and told him what she'd done to best him, she'd still be alive. He'd have taken her to bed and made her scream, given her the pain she deserved, the prod that added spice to a loving and made him come hard. Fuck, he should've agreed to a baby when she'd suggested it to him. She wouldn't have left him if they'd had a child.

Her fault.

Her fault.

Her fuckin' fault.

His heart thumped so hard, he wondered if he was having a heart attack. He forced an extra big inhalation. Slow and calm breaths and his racing pulse settled.

He needed a plan. Yeah, he'd ditch his old plan. His brain ticked over fast as a computer. He had a good brain. All he had to do was use it and find a way over or around this roadblock. And food. He needed food to aid his brainpower. The roast dinners never tasted as good as the ones at home, but it would suffice.

He had three weeks before he needed to fork over the money for the investment. The bitch had plenty of money stashed away—money she'd kept to herself instead of sharing. He had a right to that wealth. A legal right and she'd denied him.

And now, she taunted him...

A thought occurred. He twisted and tugged at the idea before a slow smile bloomed. The smile dug into his cheeks. Sexy dimples, she'd called them when they'd first met.

Yeah.

He'd done it once.

He could do it again.

The bitch owed him, and one way or the other he'd get his just rewards.

It was only fair.

Happier now that he had a plan, he stood and made his way to his rented cottage.

She'd thought she was smart. *Wrong*. He was the clever one who'd accessed her laptop via remote to learn everything he'd needed to locate her. She hadn't had a clue, and he grinned, recalling her expression once she'd recognized him.

The shock.

The sliver of fear.

Then she'd had to open her mouth, and he'd lost his temper.

That wouldn't happen again.

Never let it be said he didn't learn from his mistakes.

She'd been crying. Gerard's heart squeezed out an extra pump on seeing the red-rimmed eyes and pale face. Without a second thought, he pulled London into his arms and gave her a hug. She clung to him, and despite the circumstances, his feline purred. Gerard pressed a kiss to her forehead, most of her straight brown hair hidden beneath a pale cream beanie, then pulled back to smile at her. A matching scarf wound around her neck.

"Are you ready to go? It's cold, but it's not raining."

"I'd like to walk, if that's okay. It will help my stiff muscles."

"We never got around to that massage, did we?" He took her hand because it pleased him and led her from the bed-and-breakfast and along the garden path to the entrance gate.

"I contacted the High Commission in Wellington and found out what I needed to do."

"Aw, hell. No wonder you've been crying. I could have helped you."

"No, I needed to do it myself. I packed Jenny's stuff."

Surprise filled him and he turned to read her expression. "The cops didn't come to search through her gear?"

"No. I didn't even consider that but they should have."

"Yes. They should explore other avenues. Henry did not do this, London. I know my friend. He'd never hurt a woman. Never."

"It's okay. You don't have to keep telling me. My brain got scrambled at first, but I agree. I saw Henry and Jenny together before the race. They were happy and only had eyes for each other. Where is Geoffrey?"

"I had to leave him locked up, and he isn't happy with me. When he couldn't find Henry, he started whining and crying. Geoffrey knows something is wrong."

"I don't suppose you could take him to the police station."

"His lawyer told me they're sending Henry to Dunedin." *Not gonna happen.*

"I'm sorry."

Gerard led her toward Storm in a Teacup. "It's not your fault. Did you see anything strange when we approached the clearing?"

"No, not really. I looked for Jenny and Henry then focused on the zombies. There were a lot of them."

"Yes. I saw a zombie come out of the bush. He was big, tall, but he disappeared. We don't know his identity. The police think they have their man and aren't following up on other leads."

"How did Henry get the knife? He wasn't carrying any bags. You both wore shorts. There was nowhere for him to hide a knife. Running with one and doing the obstacles—impossible."

"His fingerprints were on the knife," Gerard said. "Henry has medical training. He touched the hilt and applied pressure to stop the blood flow, but he was too late." Gerard heard London's hard swallow and guilt filled him. "I'm sorry. This is difficult for you, but I thought you'd prefer to know the truth. Hiding information from you is the worst thing we can do."

The nights closed in fast since New Zealand was moving into late autumn. The streetlights shone on the footpath, allowing her glimpses of gardens and the shop fronts they passed.

"What is a co-op shop?"

"It's a new business, opening next week, I think. The locals can take produce or goods and sell them at the co-op shop. They receive the money less a small commission to pay for the rent and the shop assistant's wages. They will sell things from flowers and vegetables to T-shirts and pots for plants. Lots of arty people live in or near Middlemarch."

"I wish I'd made it to the craft market. Who won the zombie run?"

"A guy on the local rugby team had the fastest time. It took a while to sort out the times since the course changed for some of the runners. The winning zombie captured forty-two lives. Saber said they'd do a rerun in the spring and offer everyone who ran this race a discount on the entry fee. From what I hear everyone was happy with that and had a good time."

Gerard opened the door for her and she shivered.

"Cold?"

"No, I keep getting this creepy feeling." She glanced over her shoulder, peering into the dark and shadows untouched by the streetlights. "Ever since we left the bed-and-breakfast it feels as if someone is watching us."

Gerard shunted her inside the café and guided her toward the counter. "We have a booking," he told the young girl at the counter. "Gerard Drummond."

They waited in silence while the teenager checked the reservations then picked up menus and directed them to a private table. Once the girl left them and they'd removed their outerwear, Gerard resumed the conversation.

"What sort of creepy feeling? I didn't notice anyone."

She shrugged. "Probably my imagination."

"You thought you saw someone you recognized in the pub. Who?"

"A mistake."

"But who did you think it was?" He willed her to answer because he thought her instincts were right. He'd sensed someone too. They'd followed them at a distance when they left the bed-and-breakfast. He'd considered backtracking to find them and ultimately decided he'd keep London safe. Before they left, he'd contact Isabella and Leo. They could trail them and see if anyone followed them to the bed-and-breakfast.

"Jenny's husband," she blurted. "It looked like Royce. It wasn't though. He hates flying. No way he'd follow us to New Zealand. Even if he had, how could he find us? That's part of the reason Jenny visited this part of the world. She knew Royce would bite off his hand rather than get on a plane."

"Tell me more about Royce."

She wrinkled her nose. "Do I have to?"

"If you thought you saw him here, we need to investigate that lead. The cops aren't going to, which means we should." He interrupted when she opened her mouth to speak. "No, if there's an outside chance, we should check on his location."

"As long as I don't have to speak with him. I was going to ring him, to tell him about Jenny, but I just can't make myself."

Gerard opened his menu and studied the three available dishes. He decided on the roast pork for a change from steak. "You disliked your brother-in-law?"

"He's a control freak and uses force to get what he wants."

"Do you think him capable of murder?"

"Yes."

She didn't hesitate, a fact that surprised Gerard. "The cops check on the husband first, but this case is different because she's in New Zealand and he's in England. Do you have a contact number?"

"A number for the apartment they used to share in the city. I gave the High Commission the number. They will have contacted him. The man I spoke to told me he'd take care of the notification, although I considered calling Royce too."

"Do you have the number?"

She nodded.

"Ring it. Check he's in England." It was an order. He saw her swallow, the tremor of nerves as she reached for her handbag. "I can do it for you."

"No. I'll do it." She pushed buttons on her phone then held it to her ear.

Gerard watched her the entire time, saw her fear linger, the tension in her shoulders as she waited for this Royce to answer the call. With his feline hearing, he heard the rings. At ring eight, a machine clicked on and a man's voice said he wasn't available to take the call, to leave a message. London hung up without leaving a message.

"I'll try again later. There's a twelve-hour time difference, so he might have gone to the gym."

"You didn't leave a message."

"No, it's best if he answers. I don't think he'd return my call."

"You know best," Gerard said. "Have you decided what you want to eat?"

"Yes, I'll have the blue cod, chips and salad."

"A drink?"

"A glass of sauvignon blanc," she said.

Gerard placed their order when the waitress returned. The restaurant was busy, full of locals and a few strangers. He scanned faces of those who weren't familiar to him and met the gaze of a big man with salt-and-pepper hair waiting for a table. He nodded before turning his attention to a menu. The zombie and this guy looked as if they might be a similar height but this guy looked doughy and overweight. He didn't appear as if he could run across the street let alone wield a knife and escape with no one seeing him.

"Gerard."

He jumped when London touched him on the hand to gain his attention. "What? What is it?" He blustered to hide his surprise, his confusion. No one took him unawares in that manner.

Her eyes rounded and her expression shuttered. Hell.

"I'm sorry. I was miles away, and you made me start."

"Thinking about Henry?"

"Yes." Not far from the truth.

"You're close."

"He's my best friend, along with Sam Mitchell. I spend so much time with Henry. We were school friends and in the army together. He's my brother and my business partner. I trust him with my life."

"Jenny—we hadn't spoken for years. Three and a half years. This holiday—part of it was us reconnecting."

"What happened?"

"Royce Weaver," London said. "I met Royce when I worked in London. I only moved to Bath three years ago.

Before that I lived in London and shared the Notting Hill house our parents left us with Jenny—well, apart from the short time when I moved into an apartment." She paused while their drinks arrived. The waitress left them a basket of fresh bread, oil and dips. Once the waitress moved to a neighboring table, she continued talking. "I fell for Royce straightaway. He was charming and good looking and seemed to listen, to be interested in me." She picked up her glass of wine and gulped the first sip.

Gerard remained silent, waiting for her to continue. Not only was he interested in London and Jenny, but he wanted to hear more of this Royce. He intended to get Isabella to check him out anyway. The cops should have looked at the husband, even if he lived across the other side of the world.

"Royce acted interested in me, although I was overweight."

"You're not overweight. You're healthy."

"I am now. Then, not so much. In Bath I had little money, which meant I didn't exist on convenience food. I exercised more and lost weight. What I didn't figure out for a long time was that Royce was pumping me for information on my older sister. It was her he wanted, and his behavior toward me changed. He had his charming side and what I called his evil twin. I never knew which man would turn up when he came home from work. One night he hit me when I didn't follow an order he gave me. I-I...he hurt me. Gave me a bloody nose and my eye went black."

Fury pounded Gerard. A growl squeezed past his compressed lips and feline claws dug into his clenched fists. He inhaled and forced his feline to subside.

London frowned at him and he managed a sheepish laugh, although the lingering edges of his temper remained sharp and capable of flaring out of control if he didn't take care.

"I told him to leave." She swallowed, her cheeks devoid of color and he wanted to reach for her hand. He couldn't because claws still protruded past his fingernails. "He dragged me upstairs, kicked me in the ribs because I wasn't quick enough to climb to my feet and he... I ended up with a broken arm to go with my bloody nose and black eye."

"You should have had him arrested."

She swallowed loudly. "I wanted to forget the whole thing."

"Didn't your sister notice your injuries? Your friends?"

"Royce made sure I was isolated, and Jenny traveled often." She shrugged. "I was always an uncoordinated child, so Jenny believed Royce when he said I was the clumsiest person he'd ever met. Jenny believed I was denying my clumsiness because I was embarrassed. Royce played us both."

"I see. What happened next?"

"Royce stayed away from me, and I thanked the stars for my lucky escape. But then I realized he and Jenny were dating. They'd been seeing each other on the sly, and he'd asked her to marry him. I tried to tell Jenny she was making a mistake, that he was a violent man. She accused me of jealousy and trying to wreck her happiness. Our relationship became frosty and when she married Royce two weeks later, I knew I couldn't stay in London. A friend was moving to Bath for their job, and when she suggested I should go too, I seized the opportunity. I haven't regretted the move, but I missed my sister."

"When did you get back together again?"

"Jenny rang me out of the blue. She apologized and told me I had been right about Royce and she wanted out of the marriage. At first, I hung up on her, but she persisted. She left her job and joined me in Bath. A part of me was still angry at her. She'd shattered my trust, but she was the only family I had. Eventually, she talked me into this holiday. After three and a half years, I wanted to know my sister again—despite the past. I wanted to reconnect, so I jumped at the chance when she offered to pay our airfares.

I figured, if everything went pear-shaped, I could return to Bath."

"Lucky break for me," Gerard said, meaning every word. "If it wasn't for your sister dragging you over to this side of the world, I'd never have met you." He seized her hand, careful not to prick her with his claws. "I mean it. I like you a lot, London. It's not the right time now, but I want to get to know you better."

A blush flooded her pale visage, a tremulous smile forming on her lips.

"I promise to treat you right. I can't promise I won't lose my temper at times, but I will never strike you in anger." His gaze connected with hers. "Never."

She frowned, and his feline ceased the motorboat purring he'd started once Gerard held London's hand.

"You don't believe me?"

"What? Yes, I believe you are telling me the truth. Your eyes..." She blinked and regarded him closely.

He had to force himself not to move, to focus on batting his feline into submission. The last thing he wanted was to scare her. He'd tell her once they got to know each other better, once his human mind was sure she was his mate and his feline wasn't steering him wrong. He wanted certainty and truth between him and London. Besides, hitting on her right after someone had murdered her sister was plain tacky.

"I must be tired. I thought...never mind. It's been a long day."

Their meals arrived, delicious as normal. Gerard kept London talking and did a fair share himself as they traded personal info. She told him how her parents moved to London and conceived her there, hence her name. He described growing up in the countryside and running wild with his friends. He didn't mention the running occurred in feline form. That would come later. They finished their meal with coffee and decadent truffles.

"There is something else. When I was going through Jenny's things and packing her bags, I found a letter for me and a copy of Jenny's will. She changed it before she left London. She left me everything. Her share in our parents' house, which is let out to tenants, her jewelry and personal effects and the contents of her bank account. There was a printout along with the letter. She has...had over a million pounds in her investment accounts. I had no idea."

Gerard gaped at her, his gut bucking like a bronco intent on ridding itself of a rider. "That must have come as a shock."

"I knew she made a good living. She designed computer programs and more recently worked on apps. In her letter, she said previously everything had gone to Royce but she wanted me to have everything if something happened to her. She told me she was sorry she hadn't believed me when I'd told her about Royce and that she loved me." Tears formed at her eyes. "What am I going to do with that money? I don't need money to be happy."

Confusion clouded her pretty face, and Gerard wanted to give her a hug. "You'll work it out. Did she let you know her solicitor's name?"

"Yes, the details are in the letter."

"You should contact them and let Jenny's solicitor know of her death."

London nodded. "I'll ring them tomorrow."

The man who had stared at them paid his bill and toddled from the café, his weight making him lumber from side to side.

"He was strange," London murmured.

"I didn't think you'd noticed him. He stared, not only at us, but at the rest of the people here."

"Maybe he's a writer or an artist or something like that. We might find ourselves in a book," London said.

Gerard shrugged. "No matter what the explanation, he was peculiar."

Chapter 6

Break-In

They fought over the bill, and she ceded to Gerard once he promised her she could pay the next time. Excitement flared in her at this declaration. He seemed genuine with his interest, and if it wasn't for her sister's murder...

"I'll walk you back to the bed-and-breakfast."

"Thanks." It was darker out here, even with the streetlights. Not a single star peeped through the clouds, and the sense of being watched assailed her again.

Gerard drew her close and slipped his arm around her waist. She was grateful for the contact.

"Someone *is* following us," Gerard said in a low voice against her ear.

London flinched, her steps stalling as she glanced behind her. She couldn't see anything, but was conscious of the insidious itch in the middle of her shoulders.

"Don't look. Keep walking."

Gerard strolled with confidence, which bolstered her own, yet the bed-and-breakfast had never looked so welcoming. The owners left the porch light on for guests and it blazed in greeting, illuminating most of the garden path leading to the front door. She reached for the doorknob.

"Wait."

She froze and turned to face him.

"I want to kiss you good night."

"Oh."

He grinned at her reply. "I thought I might spot our Peeping Tom at the same time."

"Oh."

"Mostly, I want to kiss you."

She blinked at his confession, then she was in his arms, softness to his hardness, lips pressed together. Not a friendly peck. This...her mind went hazy with pleasure. Every time Gerard touched her, her body softened. Even an innocent touch of hands affected her, but this...this kiss thrilled her. He dominated her mouth, yet gave as much as he took, sending pleasure darting through her. She'd experienced nothing like it, the contact with Gerard firing each of her nerve endings. She clung, spearing her fingers through his black hair, leaving it ruffled and sexy.

He pulled back a fraction to study her reaction, his grin a thing of beauty. "Can I do that again?"

She nodded, thinking he meant tomorrow.

Not tomorrow, she realized as he dipped his head. He meant now, and his bold confidence had her clinging, dazed at the fiery enjoyment that came the second his mouth touched hers. Her lips parted, and he took advantage, sliding his tongue into contact with hers. Her breasts tingled and her mind went on a journey of *what if*?

Spears of the pleasure ricocheted and darted to her core. For the first time in ages, she wanted a man with every particle of her being. She craved naked skin and twined limbs. She craved privacy in a soft bed. She craved Gerard Drummond.

And it was the wrong time.

How could she celebrate this feeling when her sister lay dead?

Right man. Wrong place.

She'd sensed something amiss with Royce and tried to break off their relationship, yet he'd made her doubt her instincts and she'd backed away from her decision, delaying acting until it was too late. If that situation had taught her anything, it was to rely on her instincts. Everything she'd seen and experienced in the town of Middlemarch told her to trust these people, which meant the true murderer had escaped, free to do whatever he or she wished.

What would Jenny say?

London knew without a doubt Jenny would encourage her to keep living. She'd said as much in her letter.

"Hey, English, stay with me here." Gerard tickled her ribs, and she yelped and tried to break free. "A man's pride could get wounded if the lady he's kissing zones out. He might think he does wet-fish kisses, or the lady is thinking about another man. He might get a complex."

London snorted at the last because his green eyes glinted with humor. "I enjoy kissing you very much. I was thinking I'd like to do more."

His brows rose. "Like what?"

"A bed. Lose the clothes." She paused and worried her bottom lip.

"Woman, something tells me your mind turned another corner. Tell me what I can do to change it back to bed and nakedness. I look excellent in my naked state."

London laughed. She couldn't help it. She clapped her hand over her mouth to stop a repeat of the gurgling sound. The last thing she wanted was to attract attention from the owners of the bed-and-breakfast. "That's...ah...good to know."

"I bet you look sexy too. When can I prove this to you?" His left eye closed in a wink that sent blood rushing through her veins.

"You're distracting me."

"Is it working?"

"Yes. Gerard, listen. I didn't think of it before, but I don't understand why Jenny brought her will with her on holiday. Why did she bring a letter addressed to me when she expected to return home? It's not something a person takes on a holiday."

The humor in Gerard faded, and for a second, she wished she hadn't broken the flirtatious spell. "They don't."

"Yes, so the question is why did Jenny bring them with her? Had someone threatened her? Royce or someone else?"

"She said nothing to you?"

"We tried not to discuss Royce. She said she'd set things in motion to divorce him and she refused to return to him. *Ever.* She told me she was sorry for her behavior, for not believing me when I tried to tell her. I know he hit her, but she refused to tell me more. It wasn't my favorite conversation either, so we concentrated on making new memories and relearning each other. She was the sister I remembered. Lighthearted and bold. Adventurous and popular with everyone."

"Contact the solicitor tomorrow, see what you can discover. Are there friends who might know what happened?"

London nodded. "I'll ring them tomorrow. They'll want to know about Jenny. I can't face more today."

Gerard drew her into a hug, the contact driving away some of her sorrow. "One day won't change a thing."

"No."

He kissed her again, quick this time with none of the deep, drugging pleasure of their earlier embrace. He pulled away. "Would you meet me for breakfast in the morning?"

"That sounds nice. The café?" Breakfast came in her tariff but her hosts were friendly and easygoing. They never started cooking until their guests arrived since they made something different each day.

"Come and eat at my place," he suggested. "We'll take Geoffrey for his morning walk together. Not a happy camper at present. He loves Henry, but he puts up with me. He might enjoy your company better."

She smiled. "It's a date."

"Good," he said as she reached for the doorknob to enter the bed-and-breakfast. "We can discuss bed and nakedness more then."

Gerard waited until London entered the bed-and-breakfast and her footsteps receded. Someone had trailed them from the café. He hadn't glimpsed them, but he trusted his instincts and hated the idea of someone spying on them. Something to do with London because he only sensed the presence when he was with her.

He strode down the street and ducked into the shadows. Rapidly, he disrobed and stuffed his clothes in a fork of a branch. He called up his feline, allowing the shift to roll over him.

Time to go hunting.

Gerard lifted his head and dragged in the different scents, cataloging them in his mind as he worked through them, discarding some and approving of others. *London*. Yes, they liked her scent. He cocked his head to listen and retraced the path to the café.

A gruff cough came from over to his right, and Gerard slinked toward the two large pine trees. It was a man, the one he'd seen in the café.

But why would this man follow them?

Gerard settled into a crouch, confident he'd remain unseen. The man waddled but his steps were sure and positive. There was something in his fluid motion that didn't fit with the grizzled hair and lined face. His breathing was easy and not the hoarse, labored gasps of an overweight man.

He didn't feel right.

As Gerard watched, the man pulled a pack of cigarettes from his pocket, tapped one out and lit up. He dragged in several puffs and wandered toward a vehicle.

Not suspicious at all. The man had stopped to enjoy a smoke.

Once he'd climbed into his vehicle and driven off, Gerard trotted back to his clothes, shifted and dressed.

The man still felt wrong, but he didn't appear to be a threat to London.

Gerard's phone blared out its musical ring tone at two thirty in the morning. Immediately awake, his first thought was of Henry. "Yeah."

"It's London," she whispered, the words hoarse with fear.

Her terror stripped him of the remaining dregs of sleep.

"What's wrong?" He slipped from the bed, clamping his phone to his ear while he struggled into his jeans.

"Someone is trying to break into my room."

"Scream. Wake the Gibsons. I'll be there in ten minutes." Five if he didn't meet other vehicles.

He tore from the bedroom and grabbed his car keys. Geoffrey trotted after him.

"Stay."

The Jack Russell ignored him and jumped into his SUV, scrambling over to the passenger seat, the instant Gerard opened the door.

"Hold on," he said to Geoffrey as he pulled from their driveway and floored the accelerator. "This is gonna be a quick trip."

The scraping came on the window frame again along with a wooden squeak. Fear almost paralyzed her. It tightened her throat and her first scream emerged in a croak. The window rose, a big hand forcing it upward.

London darted for the door, her toe connecting with the corner of the bed. She grunted and kept going, flinging open the door. When she glanced over her shoulder, a head and shoulders appeared in the gap. She screamed, her dread rippling along the passage.

"Bitch," a deep voice snarled.

She didn't recognize the voice.

"Help!" Recalling her self-defense classes at home in Bath, she sucked in a deep breath. "Fire! Fire! *Fire!*"

To her relief, lights flicked on, piercing cracks beneath doors.

A woman in a bright pink robe—another guest—opened her door, her head a mass of rollers. "What is it?"

Mr. Gibson, her host, hurried down the passage a fire extinguisher in hand. "Where is the fire?"

"No fire. Intruder," London gasped out. "Someone is trying to break into my room."

Mr. Gibson didn't hesitate. He plunged into her bedroom, fire extinguisher still in hand. The light flicked on, illuminating the interior of the room.

London swallowed her fear and followed.

There was no one in her bedroom, but the window was half open. She hadn't imagined a thing.

"Stay here," Mr. Gibson said. "I'll check outside."

"Should I ring the police?" his wife asked.

"I think they're gone."

London heard a dog bark, a shout, then another bark followed by a growl.

"London, you okay?" a familiar voice shouted.

"Who is it?" Mr. Gibson demanded, tension giving him a rigid stance.

"Gerard Drummond," London said. "I called him first before I screamed for help."

"Anyone out there, Gerard?" Mr. Gibson asked, the rail-thin man noticeably calmer at Gerard's appearance.

"Geoffrey chased after someone. A man, I think. Geoffrey hasn't come back yet." Gerard didn't seem worried and London relaxed.

"Go to bed, Mrs. Chase," Mrs. Gibson said. "There is nothing to alarm anyone."

"A person isn't safe in their bed," the guest complained but she returned to her allocated room and shut her door with a firm click.

"I think I'll call the police anyway," Mrs. Gibson said.

"Yes, that's a good idea," her husband said. "I'm going outside to speak with Gerard."

London heard barking again. There was no way she'd sleep now. Once Mr. Gibson disappeared, she pulled on warm sweats and made her way outside.

Geoffrey barked and trotted over to her. She stooped to pat the small white-and-black dog, and he leaned into her, enjoying the attention.

"You shouldn't be out here," Gerard said when he joined them.

Geoffrey growled at him, and Gerard muttered something under his breath.

110

"Did you see who it was?" Mr. Gibson asked.

"No, but judging by his size, it was a man. He was fast on his feet. He used a crowbar to jimmy the lock."

Mr. Gibson sighed. "These are old window frames. I've been thinking of having them replaced."

"Why don't you go back to bed?" Gerard suggested. "It's cold out here."

London shivered, despite her warm clothes. "I won't be able to sleep in that room."

Mr. Gibson frowned. "We don't have another room for you to use."

"You can stay with me," Gerard said.

London nodded, not hesitating. "Yes, please." Gerard made her feel safe, and he'd come at her call. "I was moving out tomorrow anyway. My bags are packed, ready to move to the new place."

"You didn't say," Gerard said.

"It didn't come up."

"Cancel your booking and stay with me. It would put me at ease. An attempted break-in isn't so bad by itself. I mean, it's not good, but it happens. But combined with Jenny's death, I don't like it. I'd prefer to have you somewhere safe. Henry and I are security experts and not much gets past Geoffrey."

"I'm sorry it's come to this," Mr. Gibson said. "Young Gerard is right. You need to keep yourself safe. I'm sorry we couldn't accommodate you due to other bookings, but this might be best. If the room is empty, I can get to work fixing the window."

London smiled at his practical attitude.

"I'll give you a refund for tonight, since you're leaving early."

"It's okay, Mr. Gibson. You looked after me and Jenny well." She glanced at Gerard. "I'll get my bags."

Gerard and Mr. Gibson helped her with the bags, and they were soon on their way to Gerard's place, Geoffrey sitting on her lap. She stroked his wiry fur, taking comfort from his warmth.

"Did you see his face?"

"No, just an arm and shoulder. It was dark. He called me a bitch, but I didn't know his voice."

"I didn't see much either," Gerard said. "I don't like the coincidence. You need to ring home and find out if anyone has seen Jenny's ex and question the solicitor regarding the will."

"Since I'm wide awake, I can ring when we get to your place."

Gerard's house sat at the rear of a huge section. She couldn't see much in the dark, but they turned off the main road onto a gravel driveway. One side seemed to be pasture, and she caught a glimpse of a building in progress. On the other side, the looming presence of trees cast extra gloomy shadows in front of their vehicle. Gerard pulled up in front of a house with a deck.

"Home, sweet home," Gerard said. "Once we finish with our work buildings we intend to do some landscaping. Henry wants a vegetable garden, and I promised I'd help."

London followed him into the sprawling single-level home.

Aware of the time difference, she rang the solicitor first to inform him of Jenny's death and to ask several questions. After researching burial and transportation procedures, she'd decided to have Jenny interred here in Middlemarch. Her sister had talked of staying because she loved the area, so London's decision seemed right.

"She signed the new will the week before we flew out of Heathrow," London told Gerard once she'd ended the call.

He'd made them a cup of tea and they sat at a modern kitchen counter, each cupping their mugs.

"The solicitor told me she *had* put the divorce in motion and didn't want Royce to receive any of the wealth and belongings she'd amassed. Evidently, he'd made bad property investments and had wanted Jenny to bail him out. She refused."

"Is Royce entitled to any of her property?"

"The solicitor said yes. Jenny made allowance for this in the proposed divorce settlement. He'd receive their communal accounts and an apartment they'd purchased near Fleet Street. Everything else in her will is in just her name. The solicitor seemed to think that Royce can't contest the will, given they had a formal separation agreement and a divorce underway."

"Did Royce know?"

"The solicitor doesn't think so. As far as Royce knows the wills they made together during their marriage still stand."

Gerard nodded. "He knew she had money. So greed is a motive."

"So are his debts."

"Could be," he mused. "Are you going to ring Jenny's friends now?"

"I'll ring a few." She yawned. "I'm tired."

"I'll make up the spare bed for you."

"No. I thought I might sleep with you. If that's all right. I-I don't think I can sleep in a strange room on my own."

"We have top security. Geoffrey could stay with you."

The dog lifted his head on hearing his name and growled. Gerard rolled his eyes.

"I could, but I liked the way you kissed me."

There was a pause. "Just so we're clear. Will we sleep or will we do other things?"

"I am tired, so I need to sleep, but my mind was going other places." She ducked her head, cursing under her breath at the heat suffusing her cheeks. "I have no practice at this propositioning business." She peeked to test his reaction.

Gerard's lips twitched, and she got the idea he was laughing at her. She wrenched her gaze away again.

"Hey," he said in a soft voice. "I want you in my bed. Want that, but I refuse to take advantage of you when you're off-balance with all that has happened. I need you to make sensible decisions."

"Sensible, huh? I wouldn't have come with you if I'd had any doubts."

"It's been two days," he said.

"I don't work as fast as Jenny," she shot back.

There was a moment's pause before he chuckled.

"That is not a bad thing, London."

"Okay then. I'd better make these calls. I'm not looking forward to them."

The calls were worse than she'd imagined. Lucy cried. Charlotte cried. Susan cried. By the time she'd finished, her head ached, and she felt like bawling herself even though she'd wept enough. She swallowed and blinked hard to combat the nasty sting at the back of her eyes. "None of them have seen Royce, but they didn't see him often anyway."

"What about his employer? Do you know where he works?"

"Yes, at an accounting firm in Kensington High Street." She pulled up the web browser of her phone and searched for the number. A few minutes later, she was speaking to the receptionist of Hindon, Sweet, and Paxman.

"It's not him. Royce has been off work sick, but he rang today to inform them he'd be back at work tomorrow."

"Isabella said she has contacts in London. We'll give her the details you have and get her to follow up."

"What does Isabella do? How come she has contacts in London?"

"She used to live in Switzerland. I'm not sure what she did," he said. "But she has lots of handy contacts. She helped Henry and me purchase the special equipment we needed for our business."

"What does she do in Middlemarch?"

"She is in business with Caroline Rutherford. You haven't met Caroline, but you'd like her. She and her husband work at Glenshee Station, not far from Lake Tekapo. Caroline designs and makes clothes and Isabella helps her. She is starting self-defense classes for women and martial arts classes for kids and there was mention of a boot camp. If Emily is busy at the café she helps out there too."

"It's a family atmosphere here in Middlemarch. The town has a nice vibe. I understand why Jenny was so enthusiastic about staying here with Henry."

"Henry and I enjoy the community feel. To hear the elders talk, the town was dying. The young people were leaving because there was no work or entertainment for them here. The men stayed and the women moved on to other things."

"Really? I didn't notice more men than women."

"It's not as bad now. The balance between the sexes is better. Several couples have settled in Middlemarch and the town council works at the social side. Always something going on in Middlemarch."

London yawned and tried to hide the evidence with her hand.

"You're exhausted. It's been an eventful day." Gerard rinsed the mugs and placed them in the sink.

"Come on. Let's go to bed. Geoffrey, basket." He pointed to a padded dog basket and the terrier trotted over as ordered. He turned two slow circles and settled with a doggy sigh.

Bed. Nerves struck at the word, but they faded when he took her hand and wove their fingers together. His

117

touch reassured her and shoved away her unease, or at least, tamped it down. She had begged him to let her share his bed. Heat washed through her face. Sugar, she'd blushed enough in the last two days to power the entire South Island. This man made her so aware of him, yet he didn't push or demand.

Not like Royce. Nothing like Royce.

She closed her eyes as she thought of the man who had ripped apart her relationship with her sister. She'd known Gerard for two days and now she intended to climb into bed with him. With her track record, she needed to slow her pace and think.

In the bedroom, Gerard took her into his arms and kissed her, not even giving her time to catalog her surroundings.

Yeah, maybe thinking was overrated...

Chapter 7

Sweet Loving

Gerard pulled away a fraction and slid his thumb over her swollen lips. It was an intimate gesture and one that set her heart beating even faster, skipping in its normal rhythm while she stared at him. The corners of his beautiful green eyes crinkled, yet she didn't get the sense he was laughing at her.

"Why do so many of the people in Middlemarch have green eyes? It's not a common thing."

"Just coincidence." Dimples dug into his cheeks before he lowered his head again. This time, instead of kissing her, he nuzzled her neck, his lips playing over the sensitive nerve endings before he nipped the pad of flesh at the juncture of her neck and shoulder. She jumped at the sharp sensation. Not unpleasant or painful. More surprising. One of his hands slid down her back to settle on her butt.

Sensitive about that area of her anatomy, she froze and his chuckle made her blush.

"Just so we're clear. I like you. All of you. Every part of you. I wouldn't change a thing. I prefer a woman I don't have to anchor to the ground during a gusty wind."

London snorted at the vision. "Not much chance of me taking off. I enjoy my food too much."

"Nothing wrong with that. You're active too."

"Not usually. I told you I lack the sporty gene."

"Doesn't mean you're not active. And we're getting off the subject. You're not one of those woman who insist on getting dressed and undressed in the bathroom and never let me see a thing because you think you're not perfect."

London opened her mouth and closed it again, aware of the trap that lay ahead. She *was* one of those women, yet if she admitted it, she suspected Gerard would distance himself.

She wasn't perfect.

Royce had taken great delight in pointing out her flaws, yet Gerard had made his interest clear. It wasn't as if she'd stay in Middlemarch forever. Why not enjoy herself?

She wanted Gerard. *There*. She'd confessed to herself. She was more like her sister than she'd admitted.

While she'd taken the moral high ground when Jenny had enjoyed herself with a man she hadn't known for long, London wasn't much better. Her instincts told her this was a good man, although it had taken her two days to reach this conclusion. The locals liked him and he, in return, enjoyed their company and participated in the community. He was standing by his friend and taking care of a small dog who kept growling at him. Gerard hadn't pushed her to this stage in their relationship, and that more than anything, made her decision.

Her hands went to her fleece top and she tugged it over her head. "Which side of the bed should I take?"

"I didn't think you'd accept my dare."

She stopped with her fleece pants halfway down her thighs. "It's a big step for me. I trust you." She let gravity take care of her pants and they pooled at her feet. She kicked them off along with her woolen socks and smiled at him wearing her panties and the oversize T-shirt she'd been sleeping in when the intruder had woken her. "I figure Geoffrey will come if I need him."

"Huh! The mutt *would* bite the hand that feeds him. He's taken a liking to you. He'd bite my butt if you needed protection, but you're safe with me. I sleep naked. Anyone who sleeps in my bed sleeps the same way."

Another dare. The man didn't know when to stop.

He was handling her, she realized a scant second later. And doing a good job of it. If it wasn't for his silent challenges, she wouldn't have reached this point. Sugar, hadn't she decided to trust him? She whisked off her panties and straightened to tug her T-shirt over her head. As she pulled the fabric down her arms, she glanced up and met his gaze. His green eyes shimmered with sensual heat and lust.

For her.

He studied her face. His gaze stopped to trace her lips then traveled downward to her breasts. They prickled under his lazy scrutiny, not too big as Royce had complained, but perfect for her.

She'd worked at self-esteem and managed, but sometimes a brick toppled from her defenses and she stumbled. It had happened earlier but Gerard was equal to the challenge.

His attention roved on, skimming her rib cage, her waist, her wider hips to land at the juncture of her thighs. He grinned in surprise.

"You're full of surprises, Ms. Allbright."

One of those silly blushes struck her cheeks again. "Jenny dared me."

"I see you rose to the challenge. I don't think I've ever seen a woman with blue pubic hair."

"It was that or waxing everything off. I didn't want to look like a child, so I went with the blue plus strategic waxing."

"Interesting." The way he said this told her he meant much more. She'd intrigued him with this unexpected revelation.

He stripped off his clothes and drew back the covers, giving her a quick glimpse of his physique. Hard muscles and sinewy strength. A tattoo of a snarling leopard decorated his right pectoral muscle. Instantly, she wanted to wander her fingers over the masculine territory.

"Don't get a chill."

No chance of that. Not with the way his lazy gaze stroked her from head to toe and back, caressing each part of her. Heat stabbed her body. Her nipples had pebbled, due to the cold, she told herself. Sugar, who was she kidding? One look from him had her pulse beating like a wild thing, desire flaring to flash point. Aroused. Yep, she couldn't deny it.

London climbed into the bed, not with the same easy grace as him since she got her toes tangled in the covers. Her cheeks burned anew. "Stop laughing."

"I'm not laughing at you, London. You amuse me, true, but it's so much more. You intrigue me. Fascinate me. You turn me on with each of your shy, uncertain glances. I'm laughing at myself, English. You're turning me inside out. I want to pounce but I don't want to scare you."

His words rang with truth, and she liked the way he expressed himself. Yet no one could call him a chatty girl. This man was all alpha male.

"You're a deft hand at settling my nerves. I don't jump into relationships. I've told you that. With you it's different."

"Come here," he whispered, his green eyes full of challenge.

She slid across the mattress toward him, feeling sexy and desirable. He made her feel that way, like she could fly. Her breasts settled against the wall of his chest and her breath hissed out in a satisfied sigh. His muscles were hard and as she inched her lower half closer, she discovered he was hard all over. His erection pressed against her belly. Desire kicked up its heels, not taking her unawares but surprising her with the intensity. Royce hadn't affected her this way, and the two guys she'd slept with since had disappointed her, not doing a thing except leave her empty and unfulfilled.

Residual concerns floated away as she let herself drift in the moment. They hadn't been doing things the right way. This knowledge made her even more certain, and she tossed aside her prudish qualms for the last time.

She made herself a promise. Each time she let doubts flare, she'd do one thing on the list Jenny had made during the airplane journey to Australia. Each of the items scared her, but if she let doubts guide her, Royce would win. She loathed the man for the way he'd treated her and her sister and for the way he'd torn her family apart.

Facing Jenny's challenges, if she faltered, might keep her on the right path. Sugar, maybe she'd do some of the things anyway. She'd managed the bungee jump, hadn't she? The bike ride. Most of the zombie run.

She lifted her head to glance at Gerard and let her smile sink into sultry. This was London Allbright, take two, the confident woman who faced every challenge head-on. "Are you going to kiss me?"

"I didn't want to interrupt that heavy-duty thinking."

"That obvious, huh?" She added observant to his list of traits. His army training, no doubt.

"You finished? I want you to concentrate on me. On us."

"I can do that."

"Promise? I don't want to make love to a woman who isn't focused on me. You've had lots to deal with today. If you're not ready, we can wait." His lips curled. "Don't get me wrong. I want you, but I can wait."

She nodded, understanding from his tone and expression he meant every word. Integrity. She added it to her mental chart—the good traits making the pile lopsided. "I am here one hundred percent in the moment. Lying in bed with a hunky man. I'm naked. He's naked. But something is wrong with this picture because—" She let out an *eep* of surprise as Gerard pounced. He caged her between him and the mattress, his lips covering hers in a torrid kiss that left her in no doubt of his intentions.

As surprise slipped away, she curled her arms around his neck and sank into the masterful kiss. Lips, teeth, tongue and teasing. He lifted his head to stare at her and she sucked in an excited breath. What he saw must have satisfied him because he reached over to switch off the light, using the second of the dual controls, plunging the room into intimate darkness. Every sense gave her more to compensate for the loss of vision. His bigger body weighed hers down, his touch burned, setting her pulse racing. The faint rasp of her breathing seemed overloud as his wild taste filled her mouth.

His hands explored, caressed and hunted out pleasure points she hadn't known existed. Her throat, her neck, her bellybutton. The unhurried slide of his tongue over the curve of her breast. The aching of her nipple, appeased when his hot mouth sucked hard. Need rose with urgency, and when he slid a muscular thigh between hers, she moaned in anticipation.

The cooler air bathed her heated center, and he kissed then nipped the fleshy part of her neck he seemed to like so much.

"I'm going to kiss you."

"You've already kissed me."

His soft chuckle gave her pause. "Not the part shielded by blue."

"Oh."

He shifted position while her heart did that jumping-jack thing.

"I've been looking forward to this," he whispered.

The smoky quality to his voice had her wanting to please him. It was languid and lazy and seductive, leading to carnal fantasies and a tightening sensation deep in her pussy.

He raked his tongue the length of her cleft, giving a hum of pleasure. Not half as much as she was feeling, she'd bet. This...this...words failed her, so she lifted her hips to encourage more of the abrasive stimulation.

Much better than...no. Stick to the present.

He explored her slick folds with his lips and tongue and varied the sensations with puffs of warm air. Her hips jerked as he teased her clitoris and danced the sensation away. Again and again, he repeated the move until she was one raw nerve, craving satisfaction.

"Please, Gerard," she pleaded. "*Please.*"

He lifted his head, and she almost cried at the loss of contact. "Please what?"

"Make me come. W-with your mouth or...or grab a condom. You have condoms?"

"I have two boxes. I stocked up yesterday."

"Oh." *Two boxes?*

"Is that all you want to say?"

"I'm glad you had the foresight to stock up," she said in a prim tone.

He barked out a laugh. "Me too."

He rubbed his cheek against her inner thigh, the faint stubble abrasive against the tender skin. His tongue licked her clit, this time with steady pressure. She rocked into the touch, her pussy feeling empty while her clit swelled with the sweet attention. He circled her clit then passed his tongue over the swollen bundle of nerves. A rough growl vibrated in his chest, the pulsation fueling her need. She quivered in a violent spasm of pleasure, the first slow and darting all the way to her toes, a second sharp and strong enough to jolt her. A groan of pleasure squeezed past her lips as hot excitement spilled through her. Her fingernails dug into his shoulders, holding him close as she trembled in mindless abandon. Slowly, she came back to herself and pushed at his biceps.

He drew away and slid his callused fingers across her cheek. "You taste good."

She heard a drawer open and close, the crinkle of plastic and foil, then he donned the condom.

"This will be fast," he said. "A good thing since you're tired."

"Not too tired."

"Excellent." His mouth was soft against hers and pleasure at the contact filled her.

He guided his cock to her and pushed inside. His hands stroked her breasts, cupping the weight as he paused, before working his length into her. "Okay?"

"Yes," she breathed.

She felt his smile against her lips, sensed his approval as she lifted into his strokes. His hips flexed, driving him into her heat and dragging his shaft free. Even though she'd climaxed, she discovered more enjoyment in the thrusts.

He kissed her, missing her mouth and getting her chin. She giggled then sobered when he nibbled on the tender spot at the base of her neck. Every time he did that it drove her crazy. Her mind emptied of everything except him. His shaft plunged deep, his strokes faster now, his breathing heavier. The wet rasp of his tongue over that spot had her pussy flexing around his cock, and the minute tremor pulled a groan from him. His cock stabbed into her now, the sounds of arousal filling the bedroom. His big body shuddered against hers, and he froze. Her fingernails dug into his muscular back as fire swarmed over her body. Almost there. *Almost.*

Gerard groaned, pistoned his hips and stilled. His mouth sucked on that spot on her neck and pleasure swelled a little more, but she needed him to move. She almost cried when he pulled free, made a tiny whimper of complaint.

"It's all right, English." And he lifted her to his mouth again. No teasing this time, and five heartbeats later her muscles contracted and she came. The tension leached from her and he pulled away.

She lay in the bed while he wandered off to the en suite, and by the time he returned she was almost asleep. He drew her close, his arm around her waist, her backside pressed to his front. A supremely comfortable way to sleep. She smiled as he kissed her shoulder and let tiredness take her. No mistakes this time. Of that, she was certain.

Gerard slept until seven and he heard the pitter-patter of Geoffrey's claws as he came to the bedroom. He untangled himself from London and padded to the door to meet the dog. He'd want to go outside and then he'd want his breakfast. If Gerard didn't cooperate, Geoffrey would hold a grudge for sure.

Once he'd fed the terrier, he called Isabella and set that part in motion. While it seemed the husband was in the clear because of his dislike of flying, it might still pay to check some more. There had been no recent sightings of him at home in London. It might be a coincidence—an intruder trying to get into London's room—but he didn't think so.

He reached Leo and asked the shifter to put the phone on speaker so he could speak to Isabella too. He went through what had happened last night and everything they'd discovered in the will.

"I want to make sure that Royce Weaver is in London and not roaming around Middlemarch," Gerard said. "London checked with Jenny's friends, but they haven't seen him."

"Might not matter," Isabella said. "He could have hired a hit man."

"Yeah, I'd considered that. Can you find out?"

"I'll make calls. I'll know soon if there is a hit in place."

Gerard sighed, not liking someone stalking London. "Hell, I hope that isn't the case. She is my mate. I thought so before, but I'm sure of it now. I intend to keep her alive.

131

The other thing. Henry—we have to break him out of jail before they transport him to Dunedin."

"That's what Saber and the Feline council decided," Leo said. "Saber was intending to come to see you this morning. We have a plan underway, but thought it was best if you stayed out of it since you're his business partner. They'll look at you first, so you need to have an alibi. Organize a client visit or something like that for this afternoon."

"Thanks, I'll do that. I need to check a property in Queenstown. I'd put it off but the owner will see me this afternoon. She's pretty laid back, and I can take London with me."

"Do that," Isabella said. "We'll meet at the café for coffee, say around five. We should be done by then and have Henry stashed in a safe place."

"We mightn't be back until closer to six."

"No problem. We'll wait until you arrive." Isabella hung up.

Gerard made a pot of tea while he planned their day. Of course, he wasn't stupid enough to confirm plans until he spoke to London.

"Good morning." London shuffled into the kitchen wearing one of his T-shirts over her sweatpants.

"I was going to bring you in a cup of tea."

132

"I'm not good at sleeping in. Once I'm awake, I have to get out of bed."

He poured a mug of tea and added a dollop of milk.

"You know how I take my tea."

"I'm observant. Part of it is my job and army training."

Her brows rose. "And the other part?"

"I like you. A lot. I want to please you." He kept his gaze meshed with hers, a slow grin curling across his lips as she blushed. "God, that makes me hot."

"You please me." She dipped her head and his grin widened.

"Enough for you to spend the day with me? I have to go to Queenstown to visit a client. Lana Sinclair was born in Middlemarch, but she owns a restaurant in Queenstown. She's had a few problems and wants me to give her a quote for increased security. Leo and his brothers own a vineyard, which is on the way. I thought we might stop for an early lunch." Timed to coincide with Henry's breakout, but he didn't intend to tell London. Not yet.

"I'd love to get away from here for a few hours," London said, her eyes brightening. "Although, I need to make arrangements for Jenny's funeral. I've decided she'd prefer to stay here as she planned."

"If you can wait until tonight, I'll help."

"Tomorrow will do. When I rang the police, they told me they won't release Jenny's body until the autopsy is completed and the paperwork is in order. Whatever that means." A tear leaked from her left eye and rolled down her cheek. She offered him a watery smile as she swiped it away.

"I'll help. Anything you need," he repeated the offer.

"Thanks."

Geoffrey trotted inside and made a beeline for London. He leaned against her legs, offered a doggy smile and waited for her to pet him, which she did.

A phone rang and London plucked it from her pocket. She glanced at the screen. "It's Susan, one of Jenny's friends. Hi, Susan."

Gerard settled on the barstool next to London and listened closely.

"After I spoke to you, I asked around. No one has seen Royce for the last two weeks. I checked at his work, and they said he's off sick and is expected to return in three days. Evidently, he rang in this morning and told his employer his shingles have flared up again. So, I went around to his flat. The door slot is full of junk mail. The neighbors haven't seen him. The girl who lives in the basement flat told me she thought she saw him last week, but she wasn't sure. London, his flat looked empty. I don't think he's sick at all."

"Thanks, Susan. I'll mention it to the police this morning."

Gerard froze then relaxed. Dropping by the police station and casually mentioning they were on their way to Queenstown was a good idea.

"I'll double-check with his friends," Susan said. "We have mutual friends and it won't be difficult to learn if they've seen him."

"Be careful," London warned. "You know how volatile he can be if crossed. If he is sick, we don't want to spread rumors."

"I'll be careful, but if Royce has something to do with Jenny's death, he should fry in hell. You said the cops had arrested someone."

"I don't think he did it," London said. "You should have seen them together, Susan. I hadn't seen Jenny so happy for ages. Since we left England she'd returned to her normal self, but she glowed after she met this guy. I'll admit I fretted at first, but you know what she's like when...was like when she made a decision."

"She embraced it," Susan said.

"Yeah. I liked Henry. In fact, I'm staying with his friend." She glanced at him, and Gerard sipped his tea, as if he were calmly waiting for her to finish her call.

"Oh? Is he a hunk?"

From the corner of his eye, Gerard observed London's rising color. He waited with a trace of impatience, wondering how she'd reply.

"Yes. Very."

"Aha! You like him."

"I do."

"Good for you. Jenny said you didn't give yourself enough credit. When are you coming home? Are you bringing Jenny?"

"They're having an inquest, although the investigation has come to a halt since they arrested Henry. I'll wait until Jenny's body is released at least. Jenny had intended to stay here with Henry, so I think I'll have the funeral here in Middlemarch."

"I understand. We're intending to get together and have drinks in her memory this coming weekend."

"She'd like that," London said.

"Yes."

There was a silence, as if the other woman was choking back tears and trying to hold herself together.

"I'll email you and let you know how I get on with the police," London said.

"Thanks. We'd appreciate that. I'll let you know if we discover anything else."

"Be careful."

"I will."

London hung up and turned to him. "We have to go to the police station."

"I heard parts of the conversation," Gerard confessed.

She went bright red. "Which parts?"

"The important parts," he said, keeping his voice innocent. She thought he was sexy and liked him. He could work with that. "I've had a shower. Why don't you grab one now, and then we'll head to the police station. They might let us have a quick visit with Henry."

Geoffrey bounded away from his position at London's feet and barked twice.

"Are we taking Geoffrey?"

Gerard stared after the dog. It darted out the door, and from his position, he saw it skid to a halt by his vehicle. "Yes," he said. "They won't mind him at the vineyard, but he's your responsibility while I see my client. He can't enter the restaurant."

"Do you think they'd let me take him on the old steamer? I wanted to go for a ride, but Jenny said it was too tame. Will I have time to do that?"

"Yes. We'll work it out," Gerard replied. "Did you want toast to hold you until we have lunch?"

"I can wait," London said, and she stood, kissing his cheek as she passed. "Thank you." She darted away before his wits returned. Unusual for him, but she got to him that much.

"Can't I have a better kiss than that? Don't I deserve one?"

"Yes and yes," she answered from the doorway. "I'll make it up to you."

He heard her giggle and although tempted to chase after her, Geoffrey's impatient bark changed his mind. The dog was right. They had things to do. Alibis to arrange.

Chapter 8

The Escape

London rubbed her tummy as they climbed into Gerard's vehicle and gave an appreciative sigh. After their meal at the Mitchells' vineyard restaurant all was right in her world. Geoffrey settled in the rear with a doggy moan after enjoying a meaty bone. "The scallops were amazing. I even ate the orange bit. They don't serve that part of the scallop at home."

"What do they do with it?"

"I've no idea. Probably throw it away. I can't believe you ate part of Bambi."

Gerard reached for her hand as he drove toward Queenstown. Her heart went pitter-patter as it always did when he touched her. "He was delicious."

He sent her a lazy grin, as if he knew how the physical contact affected her. She hadn't expected to meet anyone and especially a man who could tempt her to change her plans.

"I'll introduce you to Lana before you and Geoffrey go on your adventure. She grew up in Middlemarch, and her cousins still live there. You'll like her. I do."

London shot him a sharp look, trying to dissect his words.

"As a friend. Leo told me her husband died, and I don't think she's ready for another relationship yet. Besides, she's not my type."

"What is your type?"

"A feisty lady with an English accent." His fingers tightened around hers and she mourned the loss of contact when he pulled away to change gear.

"You think I'm feisty?"

"I think you're gorgeous and sexy and adventurous."

A laugh slipped free. "Adventurous? Me?"

"You've tried things you've never done before during your holiday. That takes an adventurous soul."

"Even if I went kicking and screaming?"

"Anyone who ties elastic to their feet and jumps off a ledge should scream."

"Huh!" She grinned at him before she peppered him with Middlemarch questions. How cold did it get in winter? Were there many jobs available in the area? Where did they do their shopping since the shops weren't that big in the town? She was still asking questions when they parked outside Lana Sinclair's restaurant.

Lana was slim with long black hair confined in a braid and a ready smile as Gerard made introductions. She wore a white apron over her black knee-length skirt and red blouse. The apron bore a splotch of tomato sauce. She noticed London's glance.

"An accident with a plate of pasta," she said with a grimace. "I don't know why people don't keep an eye on their children in a restaurant. Can I get you something to eat?"

"We stopped at the vineyard and had lunch there," Gerard said. "London and Geoffrey are going for a walk and a ride on the steamer while we talk business."

"The chef is making cupcakes for a special function. We'll have tea and cupcakes when you get back from your walk," Lana said. "I'd love to do a trip to your part of the world one day. It will give me a chance to quiz you."

"You had me at cupcakes," London said.

"Me too," Gerard agreed.

London waved and set off with Geoffrey to enjoy the crisp day and the lake with The Remarkables mountain range in the background. Nothing better than a walk on a fine day.

They arrived back in Middlemarch late, just shy of six, after an amazing day. London had liked Lana Sinclair and felt comfortable. If she stayed at Middlemarch for a few weeks, Lana had told her they were sure to meet again, since Lana was attending one of the upcoming dances.

While Gerard had done his quote, she and Geoffrey had ridden on the *TSS Earnslaw*, an old steamer that used to sail the lake carting passengers and goods. Now, the ship sailed full of tourists.

Middlemarch was full of cop cars—well, three anyway, which was strange. London spotted several policemen questioning curious onlookers.

"What is going on?"

"I've no idea," Gerard said. "I don't feel like cooking dinner. Want a quick bite at the café?"

"That's sounds good," London agreed.

Inside the café, Leo and Isabella were eating. Gerard led Geoffrey to the outside spot reserved for dogs and filled a water bowl. Geoffrey drank then settled in a ball with a doggy groan of contentment.

"Come and join us," Leo called when he spotted them.

Gerard glanced at her. "Is that okay?"

London nodded. "Your friends have made me welcome."

"It's your English accent," Gerard whispered next to her ear.

"I think that only works for you," she whispered back.

His hand slid over her shoulders and propelled her toward Leo and Isabella. "It does. I can't wait to get you home."

The glow in his eyes thrilled her. It wasn't a line to seduce her. He meant what he said. She winked at him, heard his sharp intake of breath and smiled as she settled in one of the spare chairs at Leo and Isabella's table.

Gerard took the other seat. "What's all the excitement? We saw at least six cops."

"Henry has escaped," Isabella said.

"What? How?" London asked.

"The cops aren't saying," Leo said with a grin. "The rumor is that the on-duty cop fell asleep."

London accepted the menu a waitress handed her. "Really? But how did that help Henry? His cell was locked."

"They're saying someone aided his escape," Leo said.

A cop barreled through the door, paused, then headed straight for their table. "Where have you been, Mr. Drummond? We've been looking for you all afternoon."

"I told PC Hannah when we went to the police station this morning to inform him about Mrs. Weaver's husband," Gerard said. "I drove to Queenstown to do a quote for one of my customers."

"Who did you see?"

Gerard recounted his day and who he'd seen. "London was with me. She'll tell you," he said when the cop's expression remained skeptical.

"It's true," London said. "We haven't been in Middlemarch for most of the day. You can check with the vineyard and Lana Sinclair. I went for a ride on the *TSS Earnslaw*. I spoke with several of the staff on the steamer."

The cop took names and Lana Sinclair's phone number before stomping off.

"What a rude man," London said.

"He's in trouble for letting a prisoner escape. I don't think there has been this much excitement since the reporters descended on Middlemarch searching for the black leopards that those drunk tourists insisted they saw roaming the hills," Leo said.

"Black cats?" London said. "This town becomes more fascinating by the minute."

"Good," Gerard said and tugged on her ponytail. "Maybe we can persuade you to stay for longer."

Another cop arrived and repeated the questions. Gerard repeated his answers and the cop left.

"Is Henry safe?" Gerard asked in a low voice.

"Yes." Leo glanced at the door as yet another policeman strode inside.

He questioned them, and London glared at him. "Why are you bothering us? We've told you where we were and given you contacts to prove our alibis. I don't know where Henry is, but I am certain he didn't kill my sister. Have you checked to see where her husband is? Believe me, he *is* capable of murder."

"We haven't been able to contact him," the policeman said.

"And you don't think that is suspicious?" London demanded. "Have you checked passport details or flight logs or whatever you do just in case he has left the country?"

The policeman's mouth firmed and he stalked outside. The second he left the café, she turned to Gerard, Leo and Isabella. "All right. What is going on?"

"Henry is...has a condition," Gerard said. "He doesn't do well in captivity for long periods of time."

"You knew?"

At his brief nod, she set down her menu. "You used me."

"No," Gerard said.

"No," Isabella and Leo said at the same time.

"Look, we can't talk here," Gerard said. "You'll have to trust us."

London frowned. Good, honest people didn't go around helping prisoners break out of jail. There was a right way to do this. "You didn't consider getting bail and doing it legally?"

"They refused bail on the grounds Henry might flee," Isabella reminded her. "You know that."

She did, but hadn't thought it mattered. They'd realize Henry hadn't done the crime just as she had. What wasn't she seeing? "But-but..." London trailed off when the waitress approached. "I'll have the tomato and basil soup, please."

London caught Gerard's silent communication with Leo and Isabella, and felt a tinge of pain because they hadn't told her whatever plan they'd executed. But the truth...she might have told, since she believed in law and justice. Aiding an escape—that wasn't right.

Except, a little voice in her mind declared, the police weren't doing a good job. They weren't looking for anyone else in connection with Jenny's murder. She'd told them about Royce. She'd informed them of the intruder trying to break into her room. The policeman in charge of the Middlemarch station had dismissed her, leaving her frustrated and angry.

Gerard placed his order, and their meals arrived quickly. The other three chatted about various events in the district and discussed gossip regarding the Jessop girl who was running wild. Evidently her parents had washed their hands of her and reported her to a local council, whatever that meant.

London frowned into her soup, listening with half an ear while everything that had happened in the last few days whirled through her mind. They were right to help their friend, even if they pushed against law and order to do it. Not that she'd have handled the situation this way, but part of her understood. If it had been Jenny sitting in a jail cell… Yes, they were right to help.

"Are you ready to go?" Gerard asked.

"What? Oh. Yes."

"Good. I'll let you know how he is," Gerard said and went off to pay the bill and collect Geoffrey.

"Are you going to tattle on us?" Isabella asked.

"No." London raised her nose in the air, then felt stupid so she met their somber gazes.

"Thank you," Leo said. "Gerard will explain everything to you, and then you'll understand."

Riddles. Secrets. She'd had enough today and couldn't wait to crawl into bed. She could do without extra excitement since her stay in Middlemarch had been action-packed enough.

Gerard thought of a hundred things to say on the short drive to his home, but he said none of them. The truth. He wasn't sure how London would react to Henry's presence, and once he revealed that truth, he'd have to give her the rest.

He wanted to trust her, thought he knew her pretty well after their short time together. His feline wanted her and he, the man, desired her as he'd craved no other woman. Revealing his identity though—that was fraught with problems. It took a special woman to accept a man who shifted into a beast. Gerard swallowed, casting London a sidelong glance. He'd hoped he'd have more time, but Henry took precedence. He couldn't leave his best friend sitting in jail with the approach of the full moon.

Gerard turned into the driveway and pulled up outside the house. "Let me check in case we have an intruder."

Geoffrey barked, scrambled off London and shot out the driver's side door the instant Gerard opened it. He'd scented Henry.

"Holy sugar," London whispered, her gaze glued to something outside. "Where did that dog come from? He's huge. Shouldn't you call Geoffrey in case—"

Before she could finish Geoffrey hurtled at Henry with a joyous bark. He ran in a circle then crouched in a play-with-me stance. Gerard smiled at the little dog's excitement.

"Geoffrey knows him."

"But where was he before? He's so big. He looks like a wolf."

"That's what I need to tell you," Gerard said, his stomach bucking with those pesky nerves, even though he knew he didn't have a choice. Henry sidled closer after a wary glance at London. Geoffrey kept trying to entice his friend to play. "Come inside." He spoke to both London and Henry.

"What about the wine?"

"I'll grab it," Gerard said, pleased for the opportunity to order his thoughts. Honesty. He needed to lay out the truth. He turned away to grab the box of wine they'd purchased at the vineyard and almost dropped it when London let out a terrified squeak.

"G-good doggy," she said. "S-stay outside."

Gerard regained his grip on the box and joined London. "He won't hurt you, and he's house-trained."

Henry let out a snarl at that, and Gerard grinned. Tetchy. "He wasn't here before."

"English, go inside. He won't hurt you. I promise."

London yawned and belatedly slapped a hand over her mouth. "It's only seven thirty and I'm exhausted."

"We'll have a nightcap. I have brandy or whisky."

"A brandy sounds good. I might have a quick shower first. Is that okay?"

"Sure. Don't use all the hot water." In other circumstances he'd have taken a shower with her, but he needed to speak with Henry.

Henry cocked his head and gave a low growl. London squeaked and ran behind Gerard. Geoffrey growled, his wiry body freezing, the hair along his spine rising to attention. Gerard wrapped his arms around London as he heard the foreign sound outside too.

"Stay here," he said to London. He clicked his fingers at Henry. "Guard."

Henry growled deep in his throat, not wanting to stay with London.

"Guard," Gerard reiterated the order. "Need someone with two legs outside, bud."

Henry's growls subsided, and he planted himself between London and the door plus the windows overlooking the garden.

Gerard heard another faint scuffing outside and prowled to the door. He inched it open and let Geoffrey out before he followed. Cops or someone else? The cops would arrive in force if they suspected him of hiding Henry. Geoffrey barked, and Gerard heard a faint yelp of pain then running footsteps. Geoffrey continued to bark but Gerard called him back, not wanting the dog to get injured. The terrier came unwillingly and an instant later, a vehicle started up. Once it accelerated away, Gerard returned inside with Geoffrey at his heels.

"Someone was skulking around outside," he said. "I wonder if it was the same person who tried to break into the bed-and-breakfast last night."

"But that would mean they followed us," London said.

"Yes. Don't go anywhere alone, okay? Take one of the dogs with you."

Henry growled another complaint as he parked his butt on the kitchen tiles. Geoffrey trotted over to sit beside Henry.

"You know what," London said. "I don't think it will be safe in the shower on my own." She whipped off her pink T-shirt to show a low-cut lacy bra. "You should come and guard my body there." She dropped the T-shirt on a barstool and reached behind her to unclip her bra.

"Henry," Gerard snapped as the front of the bra dipped to reveal creamy curves.

Henry made the werewolf version of a laugh—a sort of hacking growl—and to Gerard's relief, turned away.

London stopped undressing. "Why do you call him Henry?"

Henry took the decision out of his hands and shifted.

"Because it is Henry," Gerard said and turned London in Henry's direction.

"But—" She scowled at Henry and moved closer to Gerard as Henry's change proceeded.

Soon, Henry stood in front of them. Big, human and naked.

"He's naked," London said.

"Don't look," Gerard ordered.

"I'm better looking than you," Henry said in a gruff voice.

"He's a wolf?"

"Yes, a werewolf."

"But I thought they weren't real."

Henry clicked his fingers. "Right in front of you. Careful, you might hurt my feelings."

"Is this what we needed to discuss? Did Jenny know?"

"Yes," Gerard said.

"Jenny didn't know yet, but I'd intended to tell her. We hadn't known each other long. I thought I had time." Henry's face went hard. "Car," he said and shifted to wolf and went to lay on the rug.

Geoffrey ran to the door and barked while London fastened her bra and fumbled her way through putting on her T-shirt.

152

Someone hammered on the door. Gerard recognized a voice. "Cops," he whispered.

Henry is a werewolf. This was the secret and the reason behind the jail breakout? She dragged in a shuddering breath and tried not to stare. At Henry. But her gaze had a mind of its own and she gripped the kitchen counter while gawking at the man-wolf. Henry was a werewolf...

"We have a warrant to search your house," a masculine voice said.

London watched Henry, the wolf, bristle, heard him give a low growl. Geoffrey trotted to his side and stretched out beside him. Henry curled in a tight ball, the action making him seem smaller.

"Ms. Allbright," the policeman acknowledged her while she cast a nervous glance in Gerard's direction. "I thought you were residing at the bed-and-breakfast."

"They had bookings, and I had to move. I told the other policeman that this morning."

"He didn't mention it."

And probably hadn't revealed the rest of what she'd told him either. "Why are you here? What do you want?" Anger sharpened her voice.

"We're searching for Henry Anderson, your sister's murderer. He escaped earlier today, but I'm sure you know that already."

"I heard there was a problem," she said.

"I hope we're not interrupting," the cop said, and he sniggered.

London scowled as he moved away. "What is his problem?"

Gerard's gaze swept her, his mouth twitching. "Your T-shirt is inside-out and you've got it back-to-front."

She groaned as she spied the label at her chin. "Sugar, no wonder he was smirking at me."

"I haven't seen that dog before," one cop said.

"He's old. I don't take him out much since he prefers to stay at home."

The cop skirted the two dogs. Henry kept his eyes closed, but he didn't fool London. She'd bet he was wide awake and ready to strike, should the cops make a wrong move.

The two cops returned to the kitchen after searching the rest of the house.

"Stay here while we search the outbuildings. I'll let you know when we're leaving."

"He's not here," London said in a tired voice.

"We haven't searched the outbuildings yet," the closest cop said.

"You won't find anything," Gerard said. "This is harassment. Neither of us were in Middlemarch today."

"Doesn't matter." The cop straightened, his belly leading the way as he swaggered from the kitchen to conduct the rest of his search.

London sniffed. "Those two are idiots."

"We should have a drink while we wait for them to finish."

"Good idea," she said.

They were both sipping brandy when the two cops returned, one holding a folded sheet of paper.

"Have you seen this before?" he asked.

"No," Gerard said.

"Have you?" the cop asked. "It's got your name on it."

"Me?" London asked. "No one knows I'm here."

He handed her the paper, and she spread it out on the counter. Written in block printing, the note said, *I know what you've done. You won't get away with it. I will get what is owed to me.*

London scowled at the cop. "What is this?"

"What have you done?" the cop countered.

"Nothing. I came to New Zealand on holiday, and because of my sister's murder I'm staying longer than intended." Pompous ass. London reread the note and was none the wiser. She didn't recognize the writing. She hadn't committed a crime. Sugar, she hadn't even known Gerard's friends had broken Henry out of jail until after the event.

"We're done here. If you hear from Mr. Anderson, you should contact us. It is a crime to hide a fugitive."

Both she and Gerard remained silent as the cop paused, waiting for a response.

"We haven't done anything," London snapped when it seemed as if the cop might linger. "I'm tired and could do with an early night. It's been a stressful few days."

"Call us if you learn Mr. Anderson's whereabouts."

"Yes, yes," London said when Gerard didn't answer. She could feel his tension. He didn't want the cops in his house.

The cop left and they heard a vehicle start. Henry unrolled from his ball and Geoffrey climbed to his feet.

"If you're shifting again, do it in your room and put on clothes." Gerard glared at Henry.

Henry let out a weird bark and shifted anyway. London couldn't help taking a peek. Henry was a big man. All over.

A hand shielded her sight without warning.

"Don't be a party-pooper," she complained, trying to remove Gerard's hand from in front of her eyes.

"He's worried you'll kick his arse to the door," Henry rumbled.

"You look very nice naked," London said in a prim voice. "But I like Gerard better."

"Yes!" Gerard's fingers flexed against her face. "On that note, let's take that shower."

Henry rolled his eyes. She caught the movement once she'd pried Gerard's hand away from her eyes.

"I'm sorry you ended up in the middle of this mess. I know you weren't responsible for Jenny's death."

"No, I'm not," Henry gritted out. "I asked your sister to stay with me. She was my mate."

"Your mate?"

"Werewolves mate for life if they find the right woman. Soul mates," Gerard explained.

"Yes." Henry's voice emerged with a serve of grittiness and emotion. "When I met Jenny I knew she was the one for me."

Jenny had said nothing, not that they'd had much of a chance to talk before the race. "I'm glad, Henry. It's good she was happy."

"She didn't tell me much about her husband. Had other things to discuss."

"He's a bastard," London said. "She changed her will in my favor. I found a copy when I packed her stuff."

Henry nodded. "She did say she couldn't wait to divorce him."

"Someone tried to break into her room last night." Gerard said.

"Jenny hated her husband. I know that. She said once he hit her, she knew she had to get out of the marriage. It took longer than she wanted." Henry growled. "If I get my hands on that bastard, there will be a murder."

"London checked with Jenny's friends at home. None of them have seen the man. He's not at work. Supposedly sick. No one has seen him at his flat," Gerard commented.

Henry scowled. "The bastard is here in Middlemarch, I tell you. It's the only thing that makes sense."

London froze at the chilling notion. "Here?" She'd been trying not to think of the possibility.

"Do you have photos of him? Are there any online?" Gerard asked.

London checked her watch. "I'll ring Susan after my shower. She might have one of their wedding photos since she was a bridesmaid."

"The police didn't say where they found the note," Henry said.

Gerard snorted. "They didn't seem worried. Please don't go out without me or Henry." The two men shared a glance. "Henry will be in wolf form until the cops drop the charges. At least while he's away from the house. Promise me?"

London didn't hesitate, not with the terror of someone trying to enter her bedroom still fresh in her mind. "Yes, I promise."

"I'm rested. Geoffrey and I'll take first watch."

"Thanks," Gerard said.

"Thank you, Henry." London drew in a breath, searched her heart and recalled the happy sparkle on Jenny's face, Henry's smile on the morning of the race as he gazed at her sister. "I'd have loved having you for a brother-in-law."

"Even though I'm a werewolf?"

"Um...I'm not sure my mind has registered that properly. Can I ask you questions tomorrow?"

Henry flashed a grin, tinged with sadness. "Of course. Gerard might answer them for you."

"Now I'm curious." London laced her fingers with Gerard's, the heat frisking her body no longer taking her by surprise. The physical contact comforted her and felt right.

"Now I'm worried. Thanks, buddy."

Once Henry and Geoffrey trotted outside, Gerard turned to her, concern written in his expression. "Are you okay with Henry? You're not frightened of him?"

"It might take me a while to get used to him turning furry at will. And if he shows me his sharp teeth and whispers, 'All the better to eat you, my dear,' I'll hit first and ask questions later."

Gerard barked out a laugh, but she wasn't joking. Things were bad enough without adding strange woo-woo factors into the mix. A werewolf. She'd thought them the stuff of myth and legend. Wait. If werewolves were real, did that mean—

Chapter 9

Secrets

Gerard led London into the tiled en suite off his bedroom. While he and Henry shared the house, they'd decorated their private rooms to their personal specifications. Heavily soundproofed too, to keep the illusion of privacy because they intended to share their house even after they found mates. As he turned London to face him and reached behind her to flick her bra closure, he spared a thought for Henry. He'd heard Henry and Jenny when they'd got busy in the kitchen, before he'd closed his bedroom door. They'd been happy and now sadness engulfed his friend, along with anger and a craving for revenge. His breath hissed out at the last bit.

"What's wrong?"

"We'll keep a close eye on Henry. If we find the man—person—responsible for Jenny's death, his wolf will want blood."

"Blood?"

"Revenge," Gerard said, going for truth. Best thing, he decided.

"I understand. I feel that way myself."

"How big is this Royce character? How tall?" He should have asked her earlier. He traced the loosened cup of her bra, skimming her creamy curves and reveling in her swift intake of air. "London?"

She coughed and delicate color shaded her cheeks.

He laughed and pressed a butterfly kiss to her heated skin.

"Stop distracting me."

"Can't help it." He reached past her and turned on the shower. "Strip."

"I don't react well to orders." That prissy English accent again. God, it made him hot.

"Please strip."

"Better," she said grudgingly and slid her bra down her arms. "Stop staring."

"Hard not to. You're beautiful."

She snorted, and he grasped her upper arms, turning her to face him.

"I mean every word. I wouldn't change a single thing. The man or men in your past who hurt you didn't have a clue about class and beauty. Their loss, my gain."

"Sweet-talker."

"Get naked and into the shower. I have plans for the rest of our evening."

She shimmied from her jeans and panties and sauntered past him to stand under one of the showerheads in the tiled wet room. He'd liked the idea of no cubicle and multiple showerheads to pummel his aching muscles after a hard run or a sparring session with Henry or Sam, when he was in town. Plus, there was plenty of room for two.

He crowded London closer to the wall, fitting his front to her back, and nuzzled her neck. The temptation to bite struck him like a punch—not unexpected. Not prudent either, yet he allowed his sharp teeth to scrape across her mating spot. She shuddered, her reaction not helping his restraint.

She turned in his arms and smiled up at him through wet hair. "Are we going to talk here?"

"No." A comfortable bed beckoned. "In bed, after we've made love." He never mentioned making love to another woman. With his past women, it had been about sex and feeling good, lighter. Oh, he made sure they'd had as much fun as he did. Different now. More important. Now, he cared about her reaction, her enjoyment, her comfort. If he could concentrate on something else, he'd control his demanding feline. "Let me scrub your back."

"Oh? That sounds tame."

A feline could only take so much.

He pounced, his mouth on hers, delving to taste, to dominate, to claim.

She whimpered against his lips, her arms clutching him closer. Her lush body teased his senses, her rigid nipples propelling him onward. He fueled his kiss with an erotic assault, intoxicated by her, mesmerized. The water spilled over his shoulders, her hair, yet all he could think of was getting closer, becoming as intimate as only a man and a woman could. He lifted her, rasping his tongue over her breasts, clawing tension digging at his resolution. He raised her higher and fit his cock to her entrance, teasing himself, teasing her.

She strained against him, and he slid deeper.

"Wait. London, we need a condom."

She froze in his arms, her chest heaving while they stared at each other. Her warmth and heat tore at his control. His feline snarled, the sound rippling from him, louder than the pound of the water.

Her eyes widened, her mouth rounded, and she struggled, wanting him to release her. "Who are you? What are you?"

His face. His eyes. She wriggled free of his touch and he let her. Stupid. So stupid. Why hadn't she thought, considered the ramifications? "Henry is a werewolf. You're not human either."

Gerard swallowed audibly, his throat working. He lacked his normal confidence as he stared at her.

"Cat got ya tongue?" She did not understand where the taunt came from or her bravery. He was bigger than her and could overpower her in an instant. Sugar, he'd lifted her as if she weighed nothing and supported her body without difficulty. She trusted him, sensed he'd do nothing to hurt her, yet she couldn't prevent her shudder of uncertainty.

"I'm a feline shifter," he said, his delivery flat.

A laugh spluttered free. Oh, sugar. She retreated a fraction, eyeing him with trepidation. "You're a cat?"

He straightened a fraction, his mouth firming. "I am a black leopard shifter. What's wrong? You don't like cats?"

The inappropriate humor slid from her when she realized he wasn't joking, and if she hadn't offended him, she'd come close. "Sorry."

"Do I offend you? Repulse you?"

"No, I'm sharing a bed with you. I don't...I haven't...you took me by surprise." And how. She gulped, her mind telling her to run. She took half a step when the words of a wildlife narrator plunged to the fore. *Don't run*. Running was bad. Especially naked running.

His searching gaze drilled into her as he sought the truth of her words. "I don't disgust you? You're not frightened?"

London searched her feelings. Yes, she was shocked and stupid too. Her brain should have connected the dots earlier, but he looked like Gerard again. His face and eyes were back to normal. No, she wasn't frightened.

"No, I...I have questions, of course, but I feel safe." An understatement, she realized. He made her happy, gave her balance, despite the loss of her sister. "It's just I didn't suspect..." She thought over the time she'd spent with him, with Henry and his other friends. "Your friends are shifters too."

"Most of them. Some are mated to humans."

"Who? Which ones? Have I met them?" London fired questions at him and almost laughed at his expression. She couldn't help her curiosity.

"Emily is human."

"Lisa?"

"Shifter."

"Sam?"

"Shifter."

"So don't human men get together with cat ladies?"

"Feline shifters." He paused. "I don't know of any matches like that. Mostly it's feline shifter males that mate with human females."

"Interesting." She grabbed a towel, not wanting this discussion while naked. "How many shifters live in Middlemarch?"

"Close to a hundred. There are lots of other families in the South Island. Not so many in the North."

"Are you getting out of the shower?"

"What? Ah, yeah."

London waited while he turned off the shower and handed him a towel. "You look human. Well, except for that freaky face and eye thing. I wouldn't have noticed, but I was looking right at you."

"That rarely happens. You...my control around you is tenuous."

"Why? Should I worry?"

"Because I like you a lot. My feline half wants you as his mate, and that makes him harder to control, but you're not in danger."

"A mate?"

"The human equivalent is marriage, but mating is much more. It's virtually impossible for a shifter to cheat if they're mated to their partner. Mating is like...like soul mates."

"Oh." He wanted her in that way? They hadn't known each other long, yet crazily, she was comfortable with him.

"Shifters try to stay undetected. We're capable of handling ourselves and behaving with decorum. We're not monsters."

Oops. Hit a nerve there. "I haven't run away screaming. I'll admit, you've taken me by surprise. After Henry, I should have guessed. I had no idea. No idea."

"Do you have more questions?"

"Just the one. What do you look like when you shift?"

Gerard tossed his towel into a hamper. "I thought we were going to bed."

"We are, but I want to know what I'm dealing with." Her lack of hesitation seemed to ease his tension.

"You're making me feel like an aberration."

Impulse had her trailing her fingers across his chest. "A sexy one. Please show me."

He huffed out a harsh breath and counteracted the impatient sigh by lacing his fingers with hers. A tiny shiver shimmied up her arm from the point of contact. What was it about this man? This shifter? Yes, she was giving him a hard time now, but it took little thought to understand her heart was part of the equation. Gerard had charmed his way into her heart, and not even learning of his dual nature had dented her feelings for him, not after her initial surprise. This soul mate thing...she'd need to consider this.

"I wasn't sure how you'd react," he confessed.

"Aw, was the puddy-cat scared?"

His look held disapproval as he folded his arms over his broad chest. "I'm capable of putting you over my knee and spanking away that cheek. It would make me hot."

Oops, still not a laughing matter. "Truce?"

A slow and sexy grin slid across his disapproval. "Hot sex might make it better, soothe my ruffled nerves."

"Please show me your other form."

"And then we'll have sex?"

"Then we'll make love."

He gave a quick nod. "Sit on the bed and give me room."

She gaped at him. "There's plenty of room. How big do you get?"

Gerard's bark of laughter had her grinning too.

"Oh no. Your mind did not go there."

He didn't answer but closed his eyes. As she watched, black hair sprouted on his arms, his legs, his torso. His shoulders curled inward, and his body seemed to rearrange itself. He fell forward onto all fours. She blinked, astonished at the rapidness of the transformation, and when she focused again, a big black cat sat on its haunches. The creature bore a distinctive smirk.

"I can't believe it," she said. "I'd recognize your smirk anywhere."

He growled, yet she didn't feel fear. Gerard ambled to the bed where she sat. He rubbed against her legs and let out a loud purr when she ran her hand along his spine.

"You're soft." Awe filled her at his wild beauty—the leashed power in his muscles as he moved. *Wow. Just wow.*

He rasped his tongue over the back of her hand in reply, the sensation rough, yet not unpleasant. With a final nudge of his furry head against her thigh, he stepped away and reversed the shift.

"Well? What do you think?"

"You're beautiful." Her gaze wandered his body. "In both forms."

"You could live with me? Stay with me?"

"I-I..." This was happening so fast. She liked him. She did, but she'd made mistakes before. "What about the mating process? Will something funny happen?"

"No. If you're worried, you can talk to Emily or to Caroline when she's next in Middlemarch. If we formalize our relationship, I'll bite you here." He stroked across the fleshy pad where neck and shoulder met. "It will hurt, and then it's meant to feel superb—for both of us. I don't know for certain because it only ever happens with a mate. The enzymes from my saliva will mingle with your blood and the bite will heal rapidly, but leave a raised scar. The enzymes will extend your life to match mine, and you'll heal better than you used to but you'll still be human."

"A lot to consider."

"Not really." He tugged her to her feet. "Enough talking. Yes?"

"Enough talking." She pulled his head down to meet his keen gaze. Their lips met and the resulting kiss inflamed her, consumed her. Her heart beat an unsteady tattoo as he purred his approval. He pushed her to the mattress, the sensual energy between them blazing off the charts with a few kisses. He thumbed her nipples and nuzzled her neck.

Recalling his words of mating and marking made her wet, and she parted her legs in invitation, not requiring any more foreplay. His hips ground against hers, and he muttered a soft curse.

"You push at my control."

"Is that a bad thing?"

"No," he whispered and stopped any further conversation with his lips. He groped for a condom, and moments later, he pushed inside her. "Hot. Tight. Perfect."

She smiled at him, gloried in the hunger etched into his face. London gasped at his next stroke. Hard and deep, it felt so good. He kissed her again, this one charged with sweetness, and she grew even wetter with wanting him. His thrusts increased in pace, and he nipped the marking site. Knowing what it meant now made the act more intimate, more everything. She shuddered at the sweet burn and ran her hand over his back to cup his muscular butt.

"Harder, Gerard."

He plunged into her, taking her at her word. The sweet burn flared brighter until she cried out, the piercing ache increased until the point of no return, and the entire time, Gerard held her, anchored her and stoked the fire in them both. Her climax struck, spasms rippling through her vagina, clenching his cock until he, too, fell into pleasure.

She groaned when he separated their bodies, but once he'd removed the condom, he tugged her into his embrace. He might have sharp teeth and wicked claws, but she sensed he'd never intentionally hurt her. She could tease him, snap at him pre-cup of tea in the morning, and he'd take each of her personality quirks in stride. This knowledge gave her a heady sense of satisfaction. She sighed her happiness and let sleep take her. Sheltered in his arms, Gerard made her feel safe.

He couldn't catch a lucky break. The fuckin' stars had aligned against him when his goal lingered a hairsbreadth away, so close he tasted the riches.

He winged a glare at the two dogs sitting on the deck, visible under the light of the pale yellow moon. The creatures sat like mismatched bookends. One big. One small. One white. One dark brown. Occasionally, they'd part company and walk a circuit of the house before meeting again on the deck. Both alert, as if they suspected he lurked in the trees bordering the property.

Bitch was sleeping with that guy. She hadn't put out for him that soon.

He'd asked in the local pub about the businesses in Middlemarch. The locals liked to talk, enjoyed meeting the new people who came to this one-horse town. Way too quiet for him. No entertainment. Second class.

God, what he wouldn't give for a whiff of city traffic, a glimpse of a red double-decker bus. This fresh air made him dizzy.

The dogs did their weird patrol again. Slightly different path. Enough of a difference that he couldn't make a run for it and spray paint his slogan on the SUV parked in the driveway. Real freaky, these dogs.

Time to retreat and rethink his plan. He needed a weapon, meat laced with poison or tranqs to get rid of the dogs. Tranqs probably since they'd act fast. The last thing he wanted was the sound of vomiting dogs to attract attention. Yep, tranqs it was. A knife or a gun. A knife, he decided, so he could carve that bitch's skin.

She'd never forget him if she had to wear his words carved on her skin.

Tempting, but no time to carve.

London Allbright had to die.

The next morning

"So, what about kids? How does that work?" London asked, still full of shapeshifter questions.

"The normal way. A couple has amazing sex." He waggled his eyebrows, smiling at her bubbling excitement.

"Yeah, but what are the children? Are they cat, dog, or human?"

"I wouldn't let Henry hear you call him a dog," Gerard said. "He's a wolf. Geoffrey is a dog."

"There is so much to remember. You didn't answer my question."

"When we have children, they will appear human, but they will have the ability to shift to feline. It's different with wolves. A human-wolf pairing dilutes the power of the wolf."

"What age will they shift?"

"Around early teens, but there are exceptions. You remember me mentioning Caroline and Marsh. Their son is three, and he shifted. Shocked everyone because he refuses to shift back."

"I've only known you for three days. It's too early for imaginary children."

"I explained about mates last night. There are some who click. You click with me, London. I want you. Never doubt that. Every time we make love, my feline urges me to bite you, to bestow my mark. I'm trying to give you time, but never doubt you're my other half."

"You've had other lovers."

"So have you," he countered, forcing back his feline when he yowled a loud protest. "I'll repeat what I said last night. The instant I saw you, my life changed. Touching you brings me joy. Having you in my life makes me happy. You are my mate in all ways, and I will make this official. You'll understand then, but I want to give you time too."

"Tell me about this Feline council. When do you get to shift?"

"Enough. We have today and the rest of the week for your incessant curiosity. Come here. I can think of a much better use for your sexy mouth." He glanced at his cock then at her.

She huffed out a laugh. "Typical male. It's all about the second brain."

He chuckled, the action pushing joy and happiness free. "Listen to you with that sassy English mouth. I've created a monster. You were more buttoned-up and prim when we first met."

"Sometimes I'm shy."

"Past that stage."

She made a huffy sound, but it was hard to miss the curve of her lips and the cheeky sparkle in her eyes. London Allbright was a magnificent gift, and he was having fun unwrapping the different layers.

"Come closer and kiss me."

She obeyed, draping herself over his chest and aligning their mouths until their lips almost touched. "I'm only doing this as a favor."

He placed his hand on the back of her head and guided her the last fraction. He sighed against her lips, savoring the gentle contact. Each kiss was different, each of her touches bringing a different response. Hunger. Lust. Tenderness. Love. Yeah, that was in there amongst the fun stuff.

In the past, the idea might have sent him running in the opposite direction. Not this time. As he'd told her, this felt right on every level. He took the kiss deeper and reveled in her groan, the way she gripped his shoulders and wriggled closer.

"Ride me," he suggested.

"Condom?"

A tiny part of him rebelled at having the latex between them, but he twisted his upper body free and reached for a condom.

"We can arrange for you to visit our feline doctor," he said. "He'll give you a birth control shot."

"You have a doctor? Your birth control will work for me? Do felines get sick often? Can you catch a cold?"

He slapped his hand over her mouth, and grinned at her dancing gaze. "Yes to your first two questions. Please, give it a rest. Do you want me to gag you?"

Her tongue darted out and licked his palm. The wet drag across his skin caused a chain reaction. His cock twitched, his feline gave a loud purr, and he groaned as her eyes glinted with mischief. "Please give my ears a rest."

She peeled away his hand. "Do you have sex in feline form?"

He gaped at her and ripped open the foil packet. "If both parties are feline."

"Oh. Do you—"

"Enough. If you're good for the next half hour, I'll take you to visit Emily. She is Saber's mate and human. You can pester her with your questions."

"I'd like that."

"London, remember, you can't talk to humans about this unless they're mated with a feline. You understand why we need secrecy?"

"I understand." She didn't hesitate. "I doubt anyone would believe me. I remember someone reporting mystery black cats in Dartmoor—wait! Is there a community of shapeshifters in Dartmoor?"

"Yes."

"But the Middlemarch shapeshifters come from Scotland."

"Yes." Determined to stop her questions and comments, he kissed her again. Quick. Down and dirty until they both purred. Using his strength, he lifted her, and she took him inside her heat, her gaze full of pleasure rather than mischief. She slid a hand between her legs to rub her clit as she rode him. God, she did it for him. All that messy brown hair, the blue eyes and pale skin the shade of cream. Then there was her breasts—perfect for a hand to touch and a mouth to suck—and her curvy hips that fit his hands just right.

He gripped those hips now, urged her to quicken the pace, then detonated, the pleasure so intense he thought he might have blacked out for a few seconds. She shuddered and writhed and moaned. A pretty rose color sank downward into her neck and breasts. So gorgeous.

"Mine," he said.

A flat statement of intent and ownership.

He caught her gaze, wanting her reaction.

A thump on the door broke the connection.

"Gerard. I know you're awake."

"Go away," London said.

Gerard grinned. "What do you want?"

"We had a visitor last night. Want to talk to you about it. And it's your turn to cook breakfast."

"Why doesn't he go and hunt a cow or something?"

"I heard that," Henry snapped, although Gerard could tell his friend was trying not to laugh. "Five minutes."

"He'd better make tea," London grumbled.

Gerard knew his friend had heard that too and would get things underway. "About the cow. Farmers frown upon that sort of thing, and it'd draw attention to our community."

"True," she said. "But some of the shifters are farmers."

"Who need to make a profit," he pointed out. "Come on. Into the shower with you." He lifted her off his spent cock and gave her backside a slap.

She squeaked and turned around to give him a reproachful glare. "I don't like that."

"Maybe you should remember that before you pester me with more questions."

She lifted her nose into the air, sniffed. "Questions are a method of learning." She headed for the en suite and turned to face him when she reached the doorway. "Why have you trusted me with this information? What if I approach the authorities or a reporter?"

"There has to be trust. I couldn't go further with our relationship without telling you the truth. I'm serious about you and want you to stay here in Middlemarch with me. Be my mate. You needed to know what you're getting if you stay with me."

She nodded and disappeared. Seconds later, the water switched on. Gerard closed his eyes for a second, indecision gnawing at him. Had he made a mistake? Was the feeling only on his side? He hadn't thought so, but now he wondered.

Chapter 10

Peculiar Lady

"Tea, as the lady ordered," Henry said, gesturing at the steaming teapot when Gerard and London walked into the kitchen.

"Did you get any sleep?" London didn't think so. Henry looked terrible with big bags under his eyes.

"A little. Geoffrey and I took turns dozing."

Gerard poured two mugs of tea and handed her one. He pulled two boxes of breakfast cereal from a cupboard, added bowls and a bunch of bananas.

Hungry, London helped herself to cereal and sliced a banana on top while Gerard cooked bacon and eggs.

"What happened last night? Did you see anyone?" London asked.

Gerard groaned. "And she starts with the questions again."

"We didn't see his face, but we have his scent now. He remained hidden in the trees. I kept an eye on him and let him think we didn't know he was there. That way he's more likely to return."

"Good thinking," London said. "Although the cops won't investigate a suspected loiterer."

"We're not going to tell them," Gerard said. "We'd have to tell them one of us saw someone lurking outside, which would be a lie."

London rolled her eyes at his words. "But you'll have to turn to the cops eventually. Otherwise Henry will get blamed for Jenny's death when he didn't do it."

Gerard prodded at the contents of his fry pan. "Did you recognize the scent?"

"There was that faint trace of blood again. I thought it was Jenny's blood we scented when I first found her, but maybe not." Henry looked so stricken London wanted to hug him. She contented herself with reaching over the table to squeeze one of his hands.

"Do you think she injured him?" she asked.

"We haven't learned any of the forensic details," Gerard said. "But I don't think she did. There were no defensive wounds. Everything happened fast. It needed to since she was in a race and there were so many potential witnesses. Whoever committed the crime had luck on their side."

London's brow creased. "Then what could it be?"

"He could be sick," Henry suggested.

"It can't be Royce then. The man is big and plays rugby during the winter. He likes going to the gym." She wrinkled her nose. "Another reason he hated me. I'm not a sporty person. Walking is more my speed."

"His loss, my gain." Gerard set a plate in front of Henry and another in front of her.

"I can't eat all that."

Gerard joined them at the kitchen table with his own plate. "Henry or I will finish what you can't eat."

"So what's our plan?" she asked.

"If he's decided it is safest to approach the house by the side with the bush, we can station two people there, so we can get a visual," Gerard said.

"You?" London asked. "You could climb a tree. I can't climb a tree to save myself."

"Not Gerard. He'd expect to see you and Gerard in the house. He'll expect to see me in my wolf form and Geoffrey."

"So who?" London asked.

"We'll get Isabella or Leo to hide out. Once we know who he is, we can discover where he is holing up during the day," Gerard said.

"You could keep Henry and Geoffrey inside the house tonight and give him an opportunity to come closer." London waved her fork to illustrate her point. "Let him think he has nothing to worry about then bam!" She stabbed the air with her fork. "We nab him in our trap."

"Bloodthirsty wench," Gerard said with approval.

"She has a point. If we let him get comfortable, he'll make mistakes."

Gerard's phone rang, and he rose to pluck it off the kitchen counter. "Yeah." He paused and turned to study her and Henry. "That's interesting. Yeah, I'll tell them." He hung up.

"That was Isabella. According to her contact, Royce Weaver flew out of Heathrow over two weeks ago. He arrived in Christchurch, New Zealand, ten days ago."

"That's not long after we arrived," London said. "It's him, I tell you. I mean, why would he come all this way when he doesn't know a soul here?"

"Flying to New Zealand to take a holiday isn't a crime," Henry said. "We shouldn't jump to conclusions."

"Henry is right." Gerard crunched a piece of bacon. "We need solid proof he is in the area and was here on the day of the race. If he was, we need to check his alibi. This has to be done right."

"How?" London asked in frustration. "Royce is smart. He always lands on his feet."

"You should go to the police station. You're Jenny's sister. Ask how the investigation is proceeding. Tell them you heard from friends that her estranged husband is in New Zealand. Tell them they had a legal separation and your sister intended to file for a divorce. Mention Jenny changed her will days before you left the country. Let them know how much money is involved. While you don't have proof, it's a possible motive for Royce to come to New Zealand. Remind them someone tried to break into your room at the bed-and-breakfast. Remind them about the note."

"I've done most of that already. That stupid policeman brushed me off." London's hands tightened on her knife and fork as she recalled the verbal pat on the head from the policeman.

"If he doesn't listen to you, go above his head. Ask to speak to the officer in charge," Henry said. "Contact the cops in Dunedin."

London set down her utensils and nudged her plate in Henry and Gerard's direction. "I'll make a nuisance of myself until someone listens."

"I'll drop you in town. Once you're finished at the police station, walk to Storm in a Teacup. When I've finished my quote and fitted the window security for another client, I'll pick you up. About two hours."

"I'll take my tablet and read a book or catch up on email once I've pestered the cops. I still have to organize Jenny's funeral." She turned to Henry. "Jenny told me she intended to stay here in Middlemarch, so I will see she gets her wish."

"Thank you," Henry said, his voice choked.

London swallowed the sudden thickness in her throat. The big man had cared for her sister, and she knew she was doing the right thing by having the funeral here. Jenny's final resting place would be Middlemarch. "I'll do as much as I can. Everything is on hold until the formalities are completed with the police."

Between them, Gerard and Henry ate the remains of her breakfast while she drank another cup of tea.

Gerard stood and carried his plate to the sink. "Henry, we've had work come in and need to do quotes. Some of it can be dealt with via email."

"I'll be glad to have something to do," Henry said. "I'll clean up the kitchen and plan something for dinner. Geoffrey will let me know if any strangers arrive."

Ten minutes later, she and Gerard left the house.

"Looking at Henry makes me sad," she confessed. "He seems broken."

Gerard reached across to clasp her hand as he guided the vehicle along the driveway. "Henry cared for your sister. He thought she was his mate, and he's blaming himself for leaving her alone."

"No one expected someone to grab her while she darted into the trees for a quick bathroom break," London said in a tart voice. "What could Henry have done? Jenny wasn't alone for long. Whoever did this was watching her closely, and they grabbed the opportunity. It's strange no one saw a thing. Who arranged the zombies? Was there a list of who went to each zombie territory? I thought the zombies had their own competition and entered the same as the runners."

"That's a good point. They questioned the zombies, but I wonder if there were any missing."

"Or extras," London added.

"I'll check with Saber Mitchell. He'll know." Gerard pulled up outside the police station. "You have my number. Ring me if you need me. This is Saber's number. Program that into your phone and ring him if you can't get hold of me. He's on the Feline council. You can trust him. Okay?"

London nodded and programmed in the number Gerard read out. "Can I ask him questions? About feline stuff, I mean?"

"As long as he's alone and tells you it's all right. We have to be careful what we discuss and when."

"I understand."

She released her seat belt, opened the door, and he placed a hand on her shoulder. She glanced at him with a quizzical smile. "What?"

"Don't I get a kiss?"

Her smile widened. "All you have to do is ask."

"I'm asking." His voice was gruff, his gaze drifting to her lips.

She leaned over, offering her mouth. She'd expected a quick, perfunctory kiss since he was on the way to meet a client. He curled his hand around her neck and held her in place. His green eyes danced with good humor, his mood contagious. She smiled back, her lips parted as his settled on hers. While the kiss started slow, it didn't remain that way. He tasted her mouth, ravished it, and when he lifted his head, they were both breathing hard.

"Take care, English," he said, straightening. He ran a forefinger along her nose and grinned. "Miss me."

"See you later." Her hand lingered on his biceps before she pulled away to open the SUV door.

He waved as he drove off, leaving her feeling inexplicably lonely. She shook away the emotions, telling herself she was missing Jenny. True, but she missed Gerard too. Something to consider.

She pushed open the door and entered the police station. It was a small room with no personality. Plain painted walls and a notice board covered with faded signs. A narrow bench attached to one wall, too narrow and hard for comfort. It was a room one entered and exited as soon as possible. London squared her shoulders and approached the desk.

"Is Police Officer Hannah here?"

"No, miss. He's away sick today. We have a relieving officer from Dunedin."

"May I see him please? I want to talk to him about my sister's murder. Jenny Weaver. I'm London Allbright."

"Take a seat. Officer Kelly should be able to see you soon."

After leaving the police station, London scanned the street and her surroundings for anything out of the ordinary. Two mothers pushing strollers wandered toward the café. A tractor puttered along the road, the driver pulling in at the petrol station. Shouts and screams rippled from the nearby school. Morning break for the students, and they were making the most of the fine weather.

Smiling, she continued walking toward the café. Things had gone well at the police station, better than good. The replacement officer had listened, taken notes and promised to look into Jenny's estranged husband. London had told him about her relationship with Royce, that the man was a bully and abusive. She'd departed the police station feeling lighter and confident the cops would check out the things she'd told them.

A car drove past, slowed enough to attract her attention. She tensed as it pulled to a halt, and the driver lowered the passenger window.

"Hello, dear," a blonde woman said in a husky voice. "Can you give me directions to the Sutton Salt Lake?"

"I'm sorry, but I'm not from around here. Your best bet is to ask at the petrol station or the café since the owners are locals."

"Where are you going, dear?"

London took half a step back, Gerard's warning to take care jumping to the forefront of her mind. While she suspected Royce had murdered her sister, she might be wrong. "Just to the café."

"Well hop in and I'll give you a ride."

She took another step. "No thank you."

The woman smiled, displaying her lipstick-stained teeth. "It's no trouble, dear. I'm going there anyway."

Pink. Her lipstick was bright pink. "Thanks, but I need the exercise." London forced a smile, feeling uneasy and not sure why. The lady seemed friendly enough, yet pushy too. The woman's big sunglasses hid most of her face, and it was difficult to see much with that blonde hair and heavy makeup. London turned away from the car, and tried to ignore the prickling between her shoulder blades. Sugar, her imagination had jumped to an all-time high. The lady was a tourist, not an ax-murderer. This was a public place. The tractor driver waved at her as he drove past, the driver behind him honking his horn with impatience.

London grinned when the driver of the tractor flipped off the other driver. She glanced over her shoulder. The blonde woman was scowling at her. When she noticed London's scrutiny, the frown smoothed out and transformed to a friendly smile. London's bullcrap meter twanged. Increasing her pace, she lengthened her strides to reach the café. She covered the last of the distance at a sprint, darting up the short path to the café door. She burst inside, the welcome bell jingling with the same urgency thrumming through her veins. When she glanced over her shoulder, the vehicle had vanished.

"What's wrong?" Emily appeared around the counter, wiping her hands on a white apron.

"I thought there was someone following me."

"Where?" Emily darted to the door and glanced outside. "There's no one there."

"No, I'm being silly. A lady stopped to ask me directions to the salt lake. Something about her made me nervous. She drove off."

Emily turned to her, saw the two women with the strollers were eyeing them with curious gazes. "Grab a table, and I'll get us coffee once I serve these two ladies. It's not very busy. I can sit with you until another customer arrives."

"Thanks. Could I have tea?"

"English Breakfast?"

"Perfect."

Emily hustled away and disappeared behind the counter. She returned with a tray of muffins and placed them in her display cabinet. She made coffee for the women, and they left with their takeout order.

London sank onto the wooden chair and thought back. She didn't understand why she'd overreacted so much to the woman when she hadn't done anything wrong except offer to give her a ride.

Emily came around the counter and carried over a tray bearing two mugs, a jug of milk and a teapot. She'd also included two muffins. "I didn't get time for breakfast this morning. I'm starving."

"Gerard made breakfast. I never eat much."

"Saber is always trying to feed me too," Emily said with a smile. "It's his way of showing he cares. Gerard is probably the same."

"Gerard told me about shifters last night. He said I should talk to you if I have questions."

Emily clapped her hands together. "I told Saber I thought he'd fallen for you. He told me to stop matchmaking."

"Everything has happened so fast. Meeting Gerard. My sister..." She swallowed and gave two hard blinks, hoping to stave off her tears. "Losing my sister. And now this. When I'm with Gerard everything is right and natural. It's when we're apart that I wonder if I'm crazy."

"Do you like him?"

"A lot, but I'm not sure I should trust my instincts. I've been wrong before."

A customer came in and Emily sighed. "If you want to talk between customers, you can come into the kitchen with me, although I should warn you. I'm likely to put you to work."

"Actually, I'd enjoy that. It gives me less time to think."

"How are you at making scones?"

"I have experience."

"Let me be blunt. Are your scones edible or do they emerge from the oven looking like schist rocks?"

An unexpected laugh escaped London. "My cheese scones are edible."

"Right. Now I expect you to prove it. Come on, bring your tea. I'll tell you about my life before meeting Saber. One thing about the shifter men here, they like women, lots of women," she amended and pulled a face. "But the second they meet the woman their feline wants, they don't have eyes for anyone except their mate. They're pushy and stubborn and go into bossy-mode at the blink of an eye. But they're loyal and faithful, loving and tender. Once they mark their mate, they can be possessive and jealous, but they will never, ever, be unfaithful. The feline pairings I know of are true partners. While they might be bossy, they're also supportive."

"So you've never had regrets?"

"Not for a second, but I made Saber work to win me." She grinned. "Time to make those scones. I'll serve these customers and come and help you find the ingredients."

The familiar actions of baking calmed London. She mulled over Emily's words, reassured by the knowledge Gerard wasn't playing her when he said he was her mate. Then, her mind turned to the woman outside the café. She'd overreacted, yet the woman made her uneasy. Or maybe, she was overtired. She mixed the dough with gloved hands and turned it out on the floured marble surface. After shaping the dough, she used a cookie cutter to cut rounds. She painted milk over the top, and after a final sprinkling of cheese, she placed them in the oven and put on the timer.

Emily entered the kitchen and beamed. "How are you at cookies? Do you know how to make ANZAC biscuits?"

"I've heard of them but never made them."

"It's easy enough. Just follow this recipe." She placed a tattered recipe book where London could see it. "I met Saber at the first Middlemarch Singles ball. We had sex that night, and it was the most intense..." She shook her head, humor dancing across her face. "Let's just say he talked me into staying."

"You've never regretted your decision."

"No, not once we mated. I don't know Gerard well, but I know Leo and Isabella think highly of Gerard and Henry. My sister-in-law doesn't give her trust easily. If she trusts them, I'm inclined to go with her."

"Gerard wants me to stay. Henry had asked my sister to stay. She told me before the race she was staying in Middlemarch. I told her...no, implied she was crazy. She was just out of a bad marriage, but she seemed determined."

"Do you read romances?"

London blinked at the change of subject. "Sometimes."

"Have you read the ones where the reviews complain about instalove? They scoff and say life isn't like that. With a shifter, love and relationships *are* like that. Oh, they can sleep around, but if they meet the one—their mate—it's game over. Think about it. I bet Gerard hasn't looked at another woman since he met you."

London recalled the woman who had tried to flirt with him in Queenstown. He'd brushed her aside and when she insisted on pushing her boobs in Gerard's face, he'd made it clear he was with London. At the time, she'd thought he was being polite, but now...

"What do you suggest?"

"You should stay in Middlemarch. I want to hire you to bake." Her impish grin lightened London's mind.

"I suppose I could find out about visas and such. It wouldn't hurt. I can help you this week. It will give me something to do instead of worrying about a murderer wandering around Middlemarch."

"Done. I'll pay you."

London nodded, although she guessed she didn't need the money now. Jenny had left her everything in her will. A sob broke free. Nothing was fair. She'd give away the money in an instant if it meant she had her sister back.

Why had she run?

He stared after her, anger contorting his face. When she glanced over her shoulder, he forced a smile.

Bitch.

He pulled onto the road. With London and the man away from the house, he could stake out the place better. But first, he'd grab meat from the supermarket. Might as well get onside with those mangy pooches. He had sleeping tablets at the cabin. They should be strong enough to stop those dogs in their tracks.

London bloody Allbright had been a pain in his side from the moment he'd met her. He'd made a mistake, thinking she was the one with the business nouse, the money. Still, it had turned out okay. His mistake had placed a wedge between the two sisters.

Everything would've turned out all right if Jenny hadn't changed.

But she had. She'd challenged him, mouthed off at him. Then the bitch had gone to a solicitor. She'd changed the locks and forced him out of his own home. Made him a laughingstock.

She'd refused to give him money.

He'd earned that fuckin' money.

She'd pushed him into a corner until he had one option left.

He clutched the steering wheel, his forearms tensing with the pressure.

And still the bitch had bested him.

With her dying breath.

She hadn't recognized him at first. Until he'd spoken. He'd enjoyed the way her eyes widened as she'd taken in his appearance. Then she'd turned mouthy, and he'd lost his temper. His mind had blanked, red partially obscuring his gaze. He'd yanked the kitchen knife from his concealed sheath and stabbed her in the chest. It had happened so fast. Too fast for him to enjoy the punishment he'd inflicted.

He remembered talking to her. "Should have kept your mouth shut, bitch."

She'd laughed.

As blood darkened her T-shirt and life ebbed from her eyes, she'd laughed at him.

She'd told him about her will.

She'd laughed at him, then the bitch had died.

Chapter 11

Suspicious Activity

"**A** woman visited while you and London were out," Henry said in a low voice. He stood in the kitchen and was making bread. He punched the dough and started to knead it with hard, aggressive rolls of his wrists. "She tossed meat for us to eat. Geoffrey and I made like friendly puppies."

"You ate the meat," Gerard said in a sharp voice.

"What?" London asked, appearing in the kitchen. She sat on one of the counter stools. "What has happened?"

Gerard shot Henry a warning look.

"Don't even think of hiding things from me." London bit off the words, her accent crisp and clear. She meant business, and Gerard went mushy inside. Not that he'd allow a hint of indulgence when her life could be in danger.

"A woman staked out the place," he told her.

"A woman? Do you think it's the same one who stopped to ask me for directions? Can you describe her?"

"Tall and solid. A mass of curly blonde hair. Sunglasses. White shirt with a denim skirt. Flat shoes."

"How tall?" Gerard asked, thinking back to the day of the race. He'd only seen the rear of the zombie and assumed it was a man because of his build and height.

"Close to six feet."

"So I might have seen a woman on race day. We asked the zombies about a man. What if it was a woman who killed Jenny?"

"It was a man who tried to break into my room at the bed-and-breakfast. He had hairy arms."

"What color?" Henry demanded.

"Pardon?" London said, her blue eyes full of confusion.

"What color were the hairs on his arms?"

"Not black. Lighter. Oh, Susan emailed a photo of Royce through to my phone." She pulled out the phone and brought up Royce's photo.

He had short brown hair, a toothy white grin. A kind of smugness, Gerard thought. His face was aristocratic with a faint tan and a thin, neat mustache beneath his long, narrow nose. He had trouble imagining this man with either London or Jenny. "I haven't seen him."

Henry peered over his shoulder. "Me neither."

"Could the blonde lady be a man?" Gerard focused on London. "What else did you notice when you spoke to the woman?"

Henry opened his mouth to ask questions, but Gerard raised his hand in a signal for quiet.

"It was hard to see her face because of her sunglasses. She had a lot of blonde curls—sort of untamed but tidy. She'd applied her makeup with a heavy hand. I didn't get a good look at her because there was something weird that gave me the creeps. She tried hard to get me into the car."

"What make was her vehicle?"

London pulled a face. "Dark blue. I don't know. It was a car rather than a vehicle like Gerard's."

"I didn't see the vehicle. She parked it somewhere and approached the house on foot." Henry focused on London. "How did you get on at the police station?"

"The usual guy is sick, and they have a replacement from Dunedin. He listened and took notes. He promised he'd check out what I said."

"What hobbies did Royce have?" Gerard asked.

"He likes sports, plays rugby and goes to the gym."

Henry punched the bread dough. "Anything else?"

London wrinkled her brow. "He likes to go to the theater. He told me he wanted to be an actor once, but his parents persuaded him to go into accounting because there were more, better opportunities."

"Ding. Ding," Gerard said. "That is our winner."

"If he liked acting, he might change his appearance with disguises." Henry froze, then cocked his head. "Car coming. Take over the bread, London." Henry ripped off his shirt and carted it out of the kitchen. He returned a few seconds in wolf form.

A knock sounded.

"What do we do?" London asked.

"I'll see who it is. Just pretend you're making bread."

London nodded and washed her hands before kneading the pile of dough.

Gerard returned with the policeman she'd spoken with earlier.

"Ms. Allbright." He dipped his head in welcome before focusing on her with bright eyes.

Gerard worked to restrain his growl of displeasure. That was his woman the cop was ogling.

"Did you need something? Have you found Jenny's killer?"

"Not yet. We're still combing the country for Henry Anderson. I've checked on the information you gave me this morning. Royce Weaver is in the country, but we haven't been able to ascertain his whereabouts. He landed at Christchurch airport. You say your sister had a restraining order against him?"

"Yes, and she was in the process of gaining a divorce. She'd seen a solicitor."

"He was violent?"

"Yes. I told you that this morning."

"You think him capable of murder?"

Gerard studied London's expressive face, felt her flash of fear and his feline writhed beneath his skin. His claws worked from beneath his fingernails.

"Yes, Royce is an angry man. He'll be furious once he learns Jenny changed her will."

"He could contest it since he is still her husband," the cop pointed out.

"All the assets, the apps she has designed are in her own name, and Royce had nothing to do with that part of her life. He could contest Jenny's will, but the solicitor told me he didn't think a claim by Royce would be successful for her business assets. To be honest, the news rattled me, and I haven't discussed the details with the solicitor."

"I see," the cop said. "I'll put out a watch notice for him. If you see him, please contact us. Given the circumstances, we'd like to talk to Mr. Weaver."

"I'll call you," London promised.

The bastard wouldn't get close enough to London to hurt her, let alone speak with her. Not if he had his way.

London walked the cop to the door and Gerard watched her as she disappeared into the passage. At least the cops were listening now. They'd need them later because they couldn't continue to live this way. He wanted a peaceful life with London. His mate.

"He's out there," Henry said.

Gerard pulled from his reverie to focus on his friend. "Yes."

"We have to do something."

"He's not going to kill London." The shard of pain on his friend's face was like a kick to the gut. Aching sympathy tugged at him. If London died...

"We won't let that happen," Henry said in a harsh voice. "He took Jenny from me, but I won't let him get London too. We won't let that happen."

London appeared in the kitchen doorway. "If you're discussing Royce, then I have a right to take part in the discussion."

"She's right. You're right," Henry said with a nudge in London's direction. "We need backup. Leo and Isabella. Perhaps Saber and Felix."

"Agreed. I'll call them." Gerard plucked his phone from his pocket and made calls.

Henry finished making his bread and put two loaves in the oven to bake. Gerard completed his phone calls and joined them in the kitchen. Now that they'd agreed on the plan subtle tension ramped up inside London. She couldn't sit still, couldn't settle and slid off her stool at the counter to pace between there and Geoffrey's basket on the other side of the large kitchen. Geoffrey lifted his head to study her, then issued a sigh and settled his head on his paws.

"What if it's not Royce?" London asked, her runners squeaking on the pale gray tiles to mark her progress. "What if we're making a mistake and someone else murdered Jenny?"

"English, we're not making a mistake. We will check before we take any action. If the person skulking around our property is Royce Weaver, then we'll scare him half to death and turn him over to the cops." Gerard flashed one of his charming grins, the one that made her insides roll in a good way, as he slid onto one of the four chrome-and-leather stools. "The plan worked well the first time we used it."

"You've done this before?" London asked, diverted enough to still and cock her hip against the hard corner of the counter.

"When someone was stalking Lisa, Sam's mate, we had to take matters into our own hands," Gerard said. "The guy broke into Lisa's house and attacked. He wasn't expecting two leopards, a wolf and a pissed Jack Russell to greet him along with Lisa."

"Leo and Isabella are here," Henry said as he wiped off the dusting of flour remaining on the charcoal-gray granite countertop.

Seconds later, Geoffrey barked.

"That's most annoying." London scowled at Henry.

"You wouldn't say that if Henry saved your life with those wolfish senses of his. He's saved my life a time or two." Gerard went to answer the door. He came back with all four Mitchells.

"We came together," Saber said.

"You okay, London?" Isabella asked, concern in her expression. She parked her butt on the counter stool nearest the doorway, sharp gaze scanning London, Gerard and Henry before moving on to catalog the contents of the kitchen—the appliances, the dishes in the sink and a wooden knife block. She grinned at Geoffrey who took one look at her, whined, and hid his face.

London inhaled, did a quick reconnoiter of her feelings. "Yeah, at least I will be."

"Good," Isabella said. "We will catch this guy."

Gerard's friends wore their serious faces, reminding her of soldiers in the movies with their watchful expressions. Saber leaned against the doorjamb, Felix claimed a wooden chair in the dining nook, turning it and sitting on it backward while Leo sat next to his mate at the counter. London's pulse rate jumped, and Gerard shot her a concerned glance. She forced a smile, although it didn't seem to fit right on her lips.

"You okay, English?"

"I'm fine." An understatement. She was so far from fine she felt like Alice wandering through a damp, dark cavern, following a rabbit she wasn't even sure existed. She jumped when he reached for her hand, embarrassment sinking in its claws and broadcasting on her face, yet she moved closer to Gerard, taking comfort from the physical contact.

"What's the plan?" Saber asked.

"We think he will come to the house via the bush. Henry and Geoffrey are a concern to him since he threw them meat this morning."

Isabella shot Henry a frown. "You didn't eat it?"

"It wasn't drugged. It came in a supermarket packet, and I watched him unwrap it. He's preparing the groundwork.

Next time it won't be safe to eat. Don't worry. My sense of smell is good. I'll know and Geoffrey will listen to me," Henry said.

"So we're letting him become comfortable approaching the house?" Leo asked.

"Then, we'll lay a trap and nab him," Gerard said.

"We could always put out a hit on him," Isabella commented, her voice calm as if she'd just asked someone to pass the jug of milk for her tea.

London jumped when Gerard tapped a finger under her chin. She pressed her lips together and leaned into him, scrutinizing the reactions. Saber, she couldn't read. Her gaze moved on to Leo. His handsome face appeared as stoic as his older brother's. Felix, the brother in-between, mirrored their enigmatic behavior. Henry's expression held pain—the same anguish he'd worn since his friends had broken him from jail. Isabella cocked her head, watchful and weighing emotions and responses to her outrageous suggestion.

"What if we're wrong?" London burst out, repeating her concerns. "What if it's not Royce?"

"These are the facts, English. Royce wasn't happy because Jenny started divorce proceedings. We know she changed her will, excluding him from everything except the items in the pre-nup agreement the solicitor told you they'd both signed. Royce told his work he was sick but we have proof he flew to Christchurch. Jenny is murdered." Gerard squeezed her. "The facts are adding up, London."

"He's a loose end," Isabella said in her blunt way. "He needs snipping."

London froze at the statement, then started at the *thump-thump* of Isabella's fist striking the countertop in punctuation of her statement. Wow, Isabella had a tough core of steel hidden beneath her striking blonde locks.

"London is right." Saber straightened from his lean. "We need certainty before we act."

"And if he grabs London and stabs her before we get our proof," Gerard demanded, and London heard his feline in each of his harsh words.

"Gerard is right," Henry added his opinion. "Jenny is dead. It happened without warning. The murderer is quick and not afraid to take chances. We need to protect London."

"Or he's just lucky." Saber prowled across the kitchen and stopped near Geoffrey. He stooped to pet the terrier, and Geoffrey growled in warning, his furry body tensing. Saber eyed the dog, gave a decidedly feline snarl in return and stood to face them, turning his back on a ruffled Geoffrey. "We should stake out the bush tonight and wait for him—position ourselves up in the trees—watch and only take action if he gets into the house. Get an idea of where he's staying and get a good view of him."

London could see Gerard's struggle to hide his amusement at Saber and Geoffrey's interaction.

The corners of his eyes crinkled as he said, "It's possible he's using disguises. A woman tried to get London into her car this morning."

"Make of car?" Isabella queried. "Number plate."

Gerard winked at London. "It was dark blue. A car rather than a SUV."

"Sorry. I'm not a car person. I don't own one," London said, feeling she should apologize.

"Okay," Saber said. "Gerard and London in the house. Go out for dinner and come back around nine. Give the guy a chance to get inside first. If he does, we can nab him, and keep London far away from any danger. Leo and Isabella, you station yourselves in the bush and wait for him. Find a suitable tree. The intruder will never think to look up. Felix and I will relieve you." He glanced at them. "Have I missed anything?"

"No. Sounds good," Gerard said.

"What do we do if he comes?" Felix asked, leaning forward against the back of his chair.

"If he doesn't break into the house, we'll just watch him," Saber said. "Let him get confident of his plan, whatever it might be."

"If he breaks in, we'll grab him and call the cops," Henry said.

"I think that's best. We don't want to reveal ourselves as felines, especially since you and Henry did that with the stalker after Lisa," Saber said.

Isabella sniffed. "That's why I suggested a hit. Less complicated."

Saber paused before speaking. "You're right, but I don't want too many unexplained deaths around Middlemarch either. A live catch is best. Questions? Concerns?"

"You could follow him to where he is staying and report him to the police," London suggested. "The policeman I spoke to has looked into the things I told him."

"While that is a good idea, he might escape or wriggle out of charges," Henry said. "I want to nail this bastard. He killed Jenny and he should pay."

The pain in his voice brought tears to London's eyes. She pulled from Gerard's embrace and crossed the room to Henry, wrapping her arms around him and hugging him. For a second, there was silence and Henry remained tense. But she persisted, and he relaxed, allowing her to offer him comfort.

"I think we've covered the angles," Felix said. "You said he's come to the house twice. We should scout the bush now, see if we can see where he's been hiding to watch the house."

"Good plan," Leo agreed. "Let's go."

The Mitchell men and Isabella tromped outside. London released Henry.

"You going with them?" Gerard asked.

"Thought I might." Henry disappeared and seconds later, she heard the click of wolf nails on the floor. Geoffrey scuttled from his bed to follow, leaving London alone with Gerard.

"Normally, I'd tell you off for touching another man," Gerard said. "But if anyone needs a hug, it's Henry. He takes exception when I try to hug him."

"He's frightened you'll bite." London struggled to hide her amusement. "I worry you'll bite me one day."

His eyes gleamed and went feline. His teeth were sharp when he flashed her a grin. "Count on it, English. You, I'm looking forward to biting."

Later that afternoon

The phone rang, and Gerard picked it up with a glance at the screen. "Anderson and Drummond Security." He listened to the guy on the other end, excitement filling him at another word-of-mouth job. He and Henry had been right to move to Middlemarch. Their business was taking off.

"I could come out this afternoon to give you a quote." He glanced at his wristwatch. "Say four o'clock. Five? Perfect. Thanks for calling. I'll see you then."

"A new client?" Henry asked.

"Yeah. The guy who owns the petrol station referred us." Gerard turned to London. "Want to come for a drive? We can do the tourist thing on the way and visit Sutton Salt Lake."

"I'd love to. It beats staying around here and thinking too much."

"What sort of job?" Henry asked.

"They have several cabins they hire out to tourists, and they want security lights installed. One of their guests tripped, walking from the bar to their cabin in the dark."

"Should be simple enough."

"I'll do the quote and if they give us the go ahead, I could install them tomorrow."

"I'm sorry I can't help you," Henry said, his tone apologetic.

"Not your fault," Gerard said.

Geoffrey barked, and both men glanced toward the door.

"Visitors," Henry said.

"You'd better shift."

"Should I get the door?" London asked.

"No, let me." Gerard cocked his head as their visitor knocked on the door. "Stay here, English. Henry, make yourself scarce."

Gerard strode to the door, Geoffrey at his heels. He opened the door. Hannah and his cop buddies. *Great*. "Yes, can I help you?"

"We have a warrant to search the property," Hannah said.

Gerard scanned it and cursed under his breath. He hoped Henry was listening. The cops didn't need to see him in wolf form. Not standing at his full natural height, that was for sure. "What are you looking for?"

"Who," Hannah corrected, hitching up his trousers.

Gerard stepped away from the door and gestured the four cops inside. Four, for God's sake. Talk about overkill. Once the cops entered his house, he closed the door and went to join London in the kitchen. He found London doing the dishes while Henry scrunched up in Geoffrey's basket. Geoffrey lay on the floor behind him, eyes open but demeanor calm. Henry must have communicated with the terrier, letting him know the importance of remaining in place.

The cops went through the rooms, searching for Henry. Gerard heard them opening wardrobes and cupboards, sliding open drawers. Five minutes later, they returned to check the kitchen.

"I know you're hiding the escaped prisoner. Tell us where he is," Hannah said, his gaze darting to all four corners of the kitchen.

"This is ridiculous," London snapped. "Why are you wasting your time with stupid searches?"

"We are being thorough," Hannah retorted.

London sniffed, her English accent to the fore. "Whatever. Are you finished?"

"For the time being."

"I'll see you out then," London said.

Gerard hid his smirk at Hannah's humph of annoyance. His gaze had skimmed right over Henry and Geoffrey and neither called attention to themselves.

London cleared her throat, and Hannah and his men tromped to the door. As the two vehicles they'd arrived in departed, Henry stood and stretched. An instant later, he stood naked in the middle of the kitchen.

"Do you mind?" Gerard clapped his hand over London's eyes, making her giggle.

"Those cops are idiots," Henry muttered. "I didn't kill Jenny. You believe me, don't you?"

"We believe you." London spoke for both of them, and Gerard was grateful for her certainty and belief in his friend.

"We might head out to visit the Salt Lake first," Gerard said.

"Wait, I need to get my camera."

"Grab a pair of comfortable shoes too. We have to park and walk a short distance to get to the lake."

London bounded to the door. "Walking. Good. That's much more my speed."

Sutton Salt Lake was in the middle of nowhere. Perfect for stolen privacy.

Gerard reached for London's hand and helped her over the style to the other side of the fence. Fresh air tugged at strands of London's hair and the rebel curls framed her face.

"Alone at last. We should find a quiet corner where we won't be disturbed."

"That should go against every one of my English morals, but I find the idea appealing. I've never had outside sex."

"Your wish is my command." He tugged her up a rise to view the lake.

"Is that it?"

"You sound disappointed."

"I expected..." She gestured at the drying mud, the web of cracks making the waterless lake look like a crazy patchwork quilt. "Water. I mean the lakes in England are full of water. And that smell." She used her fingers to hold her nose.

"It hasn't rained for a while. The lake is filled by rainfall and is the only saltwater lake in New Zealand. The salt comes from the soil and the way the lake is constantly filling and evaporating. Are you taking photos?"

"When I can breathe without wanting to gag."

"It's the mud. You'll get used to it soon. Let me have your camera and I'll take a photo of you." Gerard snapped several photos. "We can come back after we have rain."

"I've gone off finding a quiet spot," London said. "I've decided a comfortable bed would be better, one without this stench." She rounded a huge block of schist and came to an abrupt halt. "Gerard, that's the car I saw this morning, the one the lady was driving."

"Crap. I can't see the driver from here or the number plate. It's covered in mud."

"What are we going to do?"

"The Mitchell farm isn't far from here." Gerard pulled his phone from his pocket and made the call. He explained the situation, then hung up. "Saber and Felix have developed a sudden fascination with the Salt Lake. They'll be here in a few minutes."

"What are we going to do?"

"We'll stay right where we are and watch to see what happens."

"I don't like this."

Gerard drew her close and attempted to absorb her tremors. She'd been through so much, and didn't deserve this additional stress. He focused on the driver but could only make out a basic shape of the figure through the vehicle window. The car door opened, and the driver exited.

Every muscle in London's body tensed. "It's the same woman. I told you she was creepy. What is she doing?"

"I don't know." The figure could be a guy. They were tall enough, had broad shoulders. "Is the woman the right height to be Royce?"

"I think so. She's too fat though. Royce is solid, but he's not fat. He takes care of himself."

A growl burst from him, jealousy taking Gerard unawares. "I don't like knowing you've seen him naked."

"I wish I'd never met the man." The flat tone told him she meant every word, which appeased his feline.

"She's leaving."

"Saber should have arrived by now. I wonder what's keeping him."

The vehicle reversed from the parking area and left.

"The rear number plate is obscured too. I can't remember if it was that way this morning. She rattled me."

"It's okay." Gerard hit redial on his phone. "Where are you?"

"We would have been there, but a truck has lost its load of hay. Had to call an ambulance and the cops. Looks as if the guy had a heart attack," Saber said.

"The woman is leaving. Look for a blue Nissan. It's a rental. Number plates, both front and rear, are obscured with mud."

"Only two ways she can go from there. If the accident doesn't stop her, we'll have a better idea of where she's staying," Saber said.

"If she is staying in Middlemarch." Felix spoke in the background.

"True. London and I are going to do a quote at Gilcrest Station. We'll be home in an hour."

"All right," Saber said. "We'll let you know if we sight the vehicle. The cops have arrived, so we'll head home once the road is cleared. That should give our mystery driver time to get here, if they're intending to come this way."

Gerard ended the call and placed his phone in his pocket. "Come on. Let's see what our mystery lady was doing."

London clasped his hand with a white-knuckle grip as they made their way to the car park. Not the relaxing jaunt he'd expected. He vaulted over the fence and helped London over the style.

"There's a note under the window wiper."

Gerard squeezed her hand in silent reassurance and freed the note. "It's addressed to you."

"You read it."

He unfolded the single sheet of paper. "*You think you're safe. You're not.*" Bastard. He or she was trying to scare London and doing a good job of it.

"That's Royce's handwriting. I recognize the way he curls his F. The last one was written in block letters. I bet he did this one as an afterthought or in a hurry. We need to let the cops know."

Her tension stirred his feline, and he bit back a growl. "We will tell the cops. Ignore the note for now, and don't let Royce rattle you. You're safe with me and Henry."

"Jenny died."

Not much he could say to that.

Chapter 12

The Ex

"Royce, he-he isn't a nice man." She bit her lip and concentrated on her clasped fingers. It'd been Royce's handwriting. Her gut told her it was Royce, and cold fingers of dread trailed down her spine at the idea of facing him again.

"Don't worry, English. We're on alert."

"But he doesn't play fair. Royce doesn't follow normal rules. He plays to win."

Gerard took one hand off the steering wheel and grabbed her hand. As always, his touch allowed her to breathe, her thoughts to settle into ruffled rather than paralyzing. The more she thought about this...their plan, the more she worried regarding the outcome. What happened if someone else ended up dead because of Royce? Her thoughts veered. It had to be Royce. There was no other rational explanation for him being in New Zealand.

In the past, he'd given kudos to the country's rugby team but had nothing else good to say of the small country or the people who lived at the bottom of the world.

Her gaze kept drifting to the rear window, her stomach bucking each time another vehicle approached or pulled from a driveway.

"London, we're safe. I won't let anything happen to you."

"You can't promise that."

"I can," Gerard snapped. "You are my mate, and I will die before I let someone hurt you."

"I imagine Henry felt the same way with Jenny."

Gerard slammed on the brakes, flinging her forward. Her seat belt dug into her chest.

"You've stopped in the middle of the road."

"You've seen Henry. He'd rip off his nuts if he thought he could have Jenny back, and I feel the same way with you. It would kill me if something happened to you."

London closed her eyes, her pulse racing at the suddenness of their stop and the passion in Gerard. She needed to apologize. None of this was his fault. "I-I'm sorry. I don't know what's wrong with me."

"We'll get through this."

"I hope so."

"We will," he insisted. "Better get going." He set the vehicle in motion, an edgy silence between them.

Doubts jumped out to assault her. Was she right to stay in Middlemarch? Maybe she should leave or at least move to a secure hotel. If Royce had killed Jenny, he wouldn't hesitate to hurt her. He had a cruel streak—one she'd witnessed firsthand. She'd tried to tell Jenny, but Jenny hadn't wanted to listen.

"Stop thinking so hard. We will get past this."

"I should leave."

"No, that's the last thing you should do. I can't keep you safe if you leave Middlemarch."

The SUV pulled onto a long driveway. It curled through mature trees and ended in front of a large stone house. Mansion, really, since it reminded her of an English stately home.

"You're doing a quote here?"

"Yes. There are several tourist cabins on the grounds, and the owner wants security lights installed. Come with me. You can be my secretary."

She wanted to know more about Gerard's job, and the last thing she needed was quiet in which to worry. She studied his profile as he scanned the vicinity. Royce would hurt Gerard if he could. "Henry should be careful of Royce. He's a jealous man."

"London, if it's Royce, he won't be expecting shifters. We have the element of surprise. Trust we can keep you safe."

"You don't know him. He's vindictive."

"There's my prospective client." Gerard climbed from the vehicle and strode over to greet his client.

London followed more slowly, her mind still on Royce. Gerard didn't understand. No, he didn't believe Royce was as bad as she'd painted him.

The truth. Royce was worse.

Warm water pounded over his head as he washed away the thick makeup from his face and neck. A stroke of luck that he'd recognized the vehicle as they'd driven past the side road where he'd parked to regroup. Following them had been an impulse. A chuckle burst free. He wished he could watch her face as she read the note he'd left for her. She couldn't hide her emotions to save herself. He'd always known how to play her, and he'd played her like his grandmother's violin.

No reason he couldn't do that again.

Since the man had taken her with him, he'd played his little game and left the note before driving to the man's house. This time he'd driven right up the driveway and parked in front of the house. The dogs had watched him from the deck, neither barking but not missing a thing he did.

He'd fed them again, but they hadn't approached the steaks he'd tossed them until he'd driven down the driveway.

Tomorrow, he'd introduce the sleeping pills to the steaks, which would allow him easy access to the house.

He stepped out of the shower and grabbed a towel, roughly drying his body while he went through his plan for the following evening. Originally, he'd wanted to act this evening and get it done, but after more thought, he'd decided to work through his plan again, step by step.

It was too important to fuck up.

London Allbright stood in his way.

She had to die.

He dressed in jeans and a long-sleeved cotton shirt. When he'd purchased the steaks for the dogs, he'd added a steak for himself and a good bottle of red wine. Time to relax and go over his plan.

He padded into the small kitchenette and started to cook his early dinner. Voices came from outside, and he glanced up with little interest.

"Well," he muttered, after doing a double take. What were they doing here?

Moving out of sight, he spied on them. The man was talking to the owner of the farm and London appeared to be taking notes. The owner gestured at the far cabins, then at his. He took another step back, careful not to be seen.

A slow smile crawled across his face as a thought occurred. He didn't know why he hadn't thought of it before. Instead of entering the man's house, it might be easier to lure him out, entice him with the promise of work.

From the little he'd been able to learn, the man's business was a new one. He'd want customers. If he could find a property near Middlemarch, he'd ring the company for a quote. Even if bitch London didn't go with him to do the quote, no problem. Getting rid of the guy would be worth the effort, since it'd leave London without protection.

She'd become easy prey.

Just the way he liked it.

And if this plan didn't work, no matter since he had the other as an alternative.

One way or the other, he'd get rid of the bitch.

He'd earned that money, and damn if he intended her to snatch it from his grasp.

They worked well together, London thought, and she found the entire process of doing the quote for security lights interesting. During the trip to Gerard's house the discussion centered on his work.

"I know you said your firm intends to offer a security guard service, but I thought you were expanding slowly."

"We'll hire locals who we know, probably Leo and Isabella."

"Isabella?"

Gerard pulled up in front of his house and parked beside Henry's vehicle. The wolf and the terrier stood on the deck and watched them.

"Yes," Gerard said. "She has experience. Doug Harnon only requires guards on the gate while the movie company is in town. He doesn't want fans to enter the property and bother his guests."

"What movie are they shooting? I didn't hear Mr. Harnon mention a title."

"He didn't. I figure we'll find out if we get the job. The film crew are only in town for two nights, so it's not a big job. Henry, any problems?"

Henry growled and followed them inside. Once Gerard closed the door, Henry shifted and headed into the kitchen.

"London, eyes shut," Gerard ordered.

"It's not my fault he keeps getting naked in front of me. He has a very muscular butt."

Henry snorted at her comment. "The woman came and tossed us a steak each. Brazen this time. Parked in front of the house."

"Blue car?" Gerard asked.

"Yeah."

"She was at the Sutton Salt Lake," London said. "Left us a note. She must've followed us."

"She didn't move like a woman," Henry said.

"I'm certain it is Royce. The note was in Royce's handwriting," she added.

"He's confident," Henry said.

"Too confident." Gerard pulled two cans of beer from the fridge and handed one to Henry. "Want one, London?"

"Yes, please." She yawned as she accepted the can. "Do we have to go out tonight? I'm tired and could do with an early night."

"I need to go for a run," Henry said. "The moon is pulling me."

Gerard lowered his beer can. "You can't vocalize. Not here."

"I know. I'm not stupid."

Gerard's gaze was apologetic. "Sorry, we're on edge. London, I don't think it will matter if we stay here. I'll ring Leo and let them know."

Two hours later, she went to bed. Gerard joined her not long afterward, stripping off his clothes with quick efficiency. He slid under the covers.

"Are we arguing? You're wearing a nightie."

"I'm worried someone else I care for will get hurt. You or Henry or Isabella. Leo. Royce doesn't care who he hurts. He's greedy and self-centered."

Gerard drew her close. "Shush. Let's change the subject." He kissed the tip of her nose, making her smile. "I can think of much better things to do."

She feigned boredom while her lady parts did snappy salutes. If she kept her mind busy, she could push Royce to the background. Her right arm ached, her mind telling her to press the weakened spot of bone. No. No. *No!*

Royce kept intruding. She'd promised herself, after the big blow up with Jenny, promised herself she'd move forward, promised herself she refused to let him win.

"London?"

She rubbed her chest to ease the pressure, gave in to the urge to rub her arm where Royce had twisted it hard enough to crack the bone. "I-yes. Kiss me." *Please, give me something else to focus on.*

"My pleasure." Gerard shifted his weight over her upper body, the physical contact grounding her in the moment instead of the past. She stared up at him, focusing on his eyes. The green color deepened, the outer edges of the iris turning golden. A slow smile curved his lips, and her heart beat faster as he lowered his head. His eyes changed shape, elongating, the pupil narrowing to black slits.

Her mouth went dry, and she licked her lips. A soft growl came from him, his feline close to the surface.

"Your teeth." She hadn't noticed during their earlier encounters. "You're showing me the real you."

"You deserve to know what you're getting. I don't want you frightened of me."

"I'm not." And that was the truth. With a smile, she closed the distance between their mouths, sighing when their lips made contact. Her arms crept around his neck, holding him close. She flicked her tongue against his lips, wanting a deeper, more erotic kiss. The slow slide of his tongue against hers had a ripple effect, pushing pleasure through her. He took over the kiss, taking tiny bites from her mouth, frustratingly brief when she craved deep and passionate.

"We have the night," he whispered before he grasped the hem of her nightie and ripped it off her in one smooth motion, baring her breasts and her lacy panties. Another yank had the panties disappearing over the edge of the bed in the same way as her nightie.

"You are buying me another."

"I prefer you naked."

She tried not to laugh as she caressed his lean cheeks. The stubble tickled her palms. "Time and place, buddy."

He kissed her neck, taking nibbles of the slender column and moving downward until his tongue traced across the marking site. Every nerve in the area stood to attention, her breathing coming in quick gasps.

"I want to bite you so much."

Her throat worked in a swallow. "I couldn't stop you."

"I know." He licked the spot with his raspy tongue. "I want you to want me just as much as I crave you. You need time to get used to the idea of being my mate. You need time to understand the feline community." He sucked. "We can still have lots of fun." He dragged his tongue over her collarbone then lower to her breast. His mouth closed over her nipple, his sharp canine prodding into her breast. She shivered, the prick of pain notching up her arousal. His mouth was warm and wet around her nipple, the suction exquisite.

"Gerard." Her fingers flexed, digging into his broad shoulders. He grunted, shifting his hips and thrusting against her thigh. The tip of his cock left a wet stream on her leg.

She ran her hands down his shoulders and dug into his buttocks. His hips flexed, his cock sliding across her thigh again.

"On your hands and knees," he ordered.

She didn't argue as he moved off her, scrambling onto her hands and knees in the middle of the mattress. He moved behind her, draping his chest over her back with heat.

"Condom," she whispered.

He cursed and peeled away from her. The bedside drawer opened and closed. Foil crackled, and an instant later, he fitted his shaft to her entrance. He pushed inside her, filling her in easy increments. Clawing tension filled her at the same time as his cock.

"Faster," she ordered.

He slapped her butt as he withdrew to the tip of his penis. "My schedule."

She pushed back, embedding his cock, closing her eyes to enjoy the way he filled her.

He hissed, the puff of air stirring the hair at her nape. "Behave or I'll spank you."

"You wouldn't."

No sooner had she uttered the words, than he pulled from her and had her over his knee. He ran his callused palms over her butt, caressing the area and rubbing away the tension. His hand lifted, leaving her skin tingling. An instant later, he spanked her.

She yelped and reared up, attempting to scramble off his lap, but he was stronger. He held her easily. "The pink looks pretty." He cupped the burning spot then smacked her again.

London cried out as he repeated the blows at different angles. Quick and sharp. The pain, intense at first, morphed to something else, balanced between pain and pleasure. Another blow fell over her hot skin, then she felt his fingers. He slipped them between her legs and tested her wet center, one digit grazing her clit. She moaned and lifted into the slight pressure, silently demanding more from him.

His soft laugh and the removal of the pleasure had her groaning again. "Gerard, please."

"So you didn't mind the spanking."

"Gerard." It didn't take long for the clawing tension to build inside her. A few touches and strokes from Gerard and she went crazy with the sensations rippling at her pleasure points.

His teasing finger parted her folds, caressed but never settled. Just a delicate brush of his fingers. Torment. Plain torture.

She felt the moisture pooling between her legs and craved something to fill the emptiness inside her. As if he could read her mind, one lone finger slid inside her channel. Her pussy flexed, grabbing hold of his digit, but before she could enjoy the sensation, he pulled free.

"On your hands and knees again." He gave a light tap on her butt after he lifted her off his lap.

She followed his order and parted her legs at his gentle insistence. He filled her with one quick stroke and remained buried in her heat, unmoving. Her pussy contracted and this time he groaned. *Right.* She tightened her inner muscles, grinning at his husky groan.

"I know what you're doing," he said.

"Trying to hurry you up."

He didn't answer but withdrew and pushed inside her again with a harsh sound of animal enjoyment. Thankfully, he increased his speed, his cock seeming to grow bigger and drive deeper. His warm breath feathered her neck, and that pushed her desire higher. She noticed every touch, every sound, every frisson of pleasure.

One of his hands cupped a breast, fingers tugging a nipple. His hand wandered from her breast and between her legs. He found her clit and teased it in time with his next stroke. Hot sensual flames licked up her belly, and she sobbed out his name. "Gerard."

The velvet tension snapped without warning, shooting a coil of energy from her clit and pushing it through her body. Her channel clenched his cock in rhythmic pulses, the bolts of pleasure continuing for long seconds.

Gerard groaned and rocked his pelvis forward, plunging deep with rapid thrusts. He called out her name in a husky voice, his convulsive heave of muscles signaling his impending orgasm. He stilled, deep inside her body, his mouth feathering kisses over the base of her throat. A nip, not enough to break the skin, but to awaken her pleasure again. He purred in her ear, the feline rumble making her smile.

For long moments, they remained locked in position. Finally, Gerard sighed and pulled free. She missed his possession immediately, happiness filling her when he drew her into his embrace. Warm and replete she cuddled into him, her eyes flickering closed. Her mind blessedly empty, let her drift. Gerard murmured soft words, and she relaxed even further into slumber and started a familiar dream.

A key rattled in the lock, turned. London clutched the arms of her chair, gripping them to the point of pain.

Royce—it had to be him since no one else had a key—entered the house, the door thudding against the stop. A horn blared, and an ambulance shrieked its warning siren on nearby Notting Hill Road. Someone shouted. An instant later, the door slammed closed, the sharp crash reverberating throughout the house and cutting the sounds from outdoors.

London tensed in her favorite armchair, her gaze going to the clock above the inglenook fireplace. Ten o'clock.

"London, where the devil are you?"

She stood on trembling legs, turning to watch the door. Her mouth opened to reply. Nothing emerged except a feeble croak. She continued to stare at the doorway, her arms wrapped around her torso. Her legs trembled under the strain of holding her weight upright, her knees threatening to buckle. The steps came closer, closer, closer.

Royce appeared in the doorway, filling the space with his looming presence.

"Why didn't you answer me?"

"I-I..." She swallowed, fear rising from her belly and filling her throat, her arms dropping to her sides. Instead, she stared as he crossed the room to her in ground-eating steps.

The scent of alcohol wafted toward her, nauseating and worrying.

"Speak," he ordered. "Why didn't you answer me?"

"I didn't hear you." Her timid lie barely reached him, but she knew he'd heard.

His full lips twisted in a sneer. "Where is my dinner?"

"In the fridge. It will need heating." She forced a watery smile, her chest so tight she had trouble drawing a breath.

"I told you I wanted it on the table ready for me when I arrived home."

He never invited her out to meet his friends, treating her like an embarrassing convenience. He berated her for being fat and insisted that she diet. After this morning's lecture, she'd had enough. She'd decided he could have the same meal as her—something low on calories. A silly time for her to gain bravery.

"I didn't k-know when you'd be home."

"I want my dinner." His gaze slid down her body.

She wanted to wrap her arms around herself again, but remained motionless because she knew the less she reacted, the better.

"All right. It won't take me long." She sidled past him, scurrying into the passage and toward the kitchen before he could grab her. In this mood he was unpredictable. Drunk, but not too drunk.

He'd hit her last week when she hadn't moved fast enough to follow his order. She couldn't even remember what she'd done to annoy him now. But the bruise on her left cheek was still healing beneath the heavy layer of makeup.

She removed the meal from the fridge and placed it in the microwave, putting the timer on for three minutes. Maybe he wouldn't notice the lack of calories since she'd added his favorite mashed potatoes. She could add a serving of baked beans. He liked baked beans. Yes. Yes, she'd do that now. Open a tin and add them to bulk out his meal.

Heavy footsteps approached the kitchen. Her breath caught, tension swelling in her again. She had to force herself to move to the pantry, to retrieve the can of baked beans. Her hands trembled as she opened the can and added a portion to the plate before setting the microwave again.

Royce sat at the table, waiting for his meal. She watched the timer on the microwave, willing it to count down before he barked at her. She didn't look at him, merely willed the microwave to hurry. *Finally,* finally *the timer dinged. She opened the door and lifted out the plate. The contents burned her hands, but she didn't murmur a sound, merely placing the plate on the table.*

She couldn't continue this way.

She didn't love him any longer, wondered if she'd ever loved him.

Somehow, he'd ended up moving in and leaving her to pay the bills. Whenever she asked him to help and to pay a share, he flipped his lid. Jenny would ask—no. He was here because of her, and she had to get the money from him and get him to leave.

All she had to do was steel her nerve and tell him.

"I want sex tonight."

"No." The refusal escaped before she even thought about reacting to his demands.

His head snapped up, fury blazing in his eyes, pulling his facial muscles taut. "What did you say?"

Sugar, she'd done it now. "I said no. I don't want you here. I want you to move out."

He stood, his big, muscular frame looming over her. He grabbed her by the shoulders and shook her. When he stopped, her head whirled, her thoughts spinning in a muddy mess.

"Don't tell me what to do." He gripped her right arm and dragged her from the kitchen. Agony tore through her arm. She tried to dig in her heels but she was no match for his strength. She belted her hip on a sideboard and cried out. Royce didn't stop. He continued to yank her toward the flight of stairs leading to the upper floor. She stubbed her toe and tripped on the stairs. Royce still didn't stop until he reached her bedroom.

Tears streamed down her eyes, blurring her vision. He threw her on the bed, not caring he'd hurt her, that her arm throbbed in discomfort.

Instead, he stood and unfastened his belt, yanking it from his belt loops.

London screamed as he lifted his arm, tried to scramble away.

She screamed again as the belt buckle bit into her flesh. Pain tore through her shoulder, her ribs with each blow. He cursed at her, called her a whore and a bitch. She screamed at the flare of agony. She screamed at the stinging, hammering blows. London screamed until her throat burned but he didn't stop.

He didn't stop.

"London. *London.*"

She bolted upright, her chest hurting, aching, her eyes squinting in defense against the bright light. A dog barked. Another growled, piercing her confusion.

"London, what is it?"

The concern pierced her panic, but she flinched at a movement to her right.

Her eyes focused, and she realized tears wet her cheeks.

Gerard sat on the side of the bed. "English, what's wrong? You were screaming."

The bedroom door flew open and Henry burst inside. Geoffrey scampered in after Henry, the fur bristling along his spine.

Henry's gaze went to all four corners of the bedroom before focusing on her and Gerard.

"I had a bad dream," London said. Not so much a dream as a memory.

"Everything okay?" Henry asked.

"Yeah, thanks," Gerard said.

Henry and Geoffrey left the bedroom and Henry closed the door after them.

"I'm sorry I woke you." She couldn't meet his gaze, not when the past filled her mind with renewed horror.

Gerard reached for her hand and wove their fingers together. "Want to talk?"

Not really. "I dreamed Royce was hitting me with his belt." Not quite what she'd meant to say. She hadn't had this dream for a long time. Thank goodness she'd woken before it had become worse. Much worse. "I'm sorry."

"You have nothing to be sorry for. Do you want to lie back down, or would you like to get up and have a whisky?"

She shuddered at the idea of closing her eyes, seeing the slow-running video repeat in her mind. "Whisky."

"Okay." He stood and pulled on a pair of jeans.

"You don't have to get up too."

"You're my mate," he said in a firm voice. "You were talking in your sleep, then you screamed. I could feel your terror." He padded around to her side of the bed and cupped her face in his hands. "I'm sensing this wasn't simply a bad dream. I hope you'll talk to me, tell me what happened."

Her breaths rasped in and out, in and out, and she wanted to run and hide, find a safe place. Instead, she stood in Gerard's loose embrace and trembled. His big hand rubbed her spine until her tremors eased. "It was seeing Royce again. I-I know it was him. The note. He's trying to s-scare me, make me remember."

"What is he trying to get you to remember?"

"That he's bigger and stronger than me."

His hand smoothed over her hair. "What did he do to you, London?"

"He-he beat me." She tried to pull away, but he held her with his gentleness. She sneaked a quick glance at his face before focusing on her bare feet. Her toenails were still bright pink from the pedicure she and Jenny had done in Queenstown. To celebrate their bungee jump. Her eyes filled with tears at the thought of her sister. Royce had killed her.

Gerard released her and picked up his discarded T-shirt. "Lift your arms for me."

Like a wooden doll, she obeyed, raising her arms over her head. He drew her arms through the sleeves and tugged the T-shirt over her head, smoothing the soft fabric over her torso. His scent surrounded her, soothed her lingering fears.

Gerard handed her a pair of sweat pants, and he helped her balance as she stepped into them. Once she'd dressed, he took her hand again and led her from the bedroom to the kitchen. He switched on a light and shunted her to a stool at the breakfast bar. "Sit there while I get us whisky."

She slid onto the stool and hunched over, periodically shivering. She wrapped her arms around herself to warm her chilled limbs.

"Here you go." Gerard handed her a tumbler of whisky and rounded the counter to sit on the stool beside her.

London wrapped her hand around the glass and took a sip. The peaty flavor burst across her taste buds as she swallowed the liquid. It warmed all the way down her throat. She risked a glance at Gerard. He smiled at her, his expression containing infinite patience.

"What did he do to you, English? You mentioned he took up with your sister and married her, but there's more, isn't there?"

She gave a jerky nod, her mind shuddering at revisiting this past. But she couldn't let Royce win, and not telling Gerard, a man who cared for her, would mean Royce emerged the victor. She swallowed and swallowed again to rid herself of the lump in her throat. "He broke my arm, and he raped me."

Chapter 13

Encounter from the Past

"The bastard raped her," Gerard told Henry the next morning. He filled the jug and hit the on-off button. "He beat her, broke her arm and raped her, then moved on to Jenny. London said Jenny didn't believe her when she tried to warn her, that she didn't see evidence of the beatings he gave London because Jenny traveled a lot for her work. He isolated London and covered all his bases, did the groundwork, and broke London's spirit. Bastard told Jenny that London would try to make trouble, and Jenny didn't believe London. Jenny thought London was jealous and would say anything to break them up. The sisters had an argument, and London moved to Bath.

"They didn't speak again until just before their trip to Australia and New Zealand. Jenny contacted London and apologized. London said she hung up on her sister at first, but that Jenny persisted and went to Bath." Gerard shook his head, angry on London's behalf but wary of attacking Jenny too much in Henry's presence. "London made Jenny work for forgiveness. She spent two weeks in Bath, approaching London every day and telling her how sorry she was about letting a man come between them. London said that although her sister had hurt her and she was still angry, Jenny was the only family she had left, so she finally agreed to this trip, taking one day at a time. Jenny told London she'd seen a solicitor and had started divorce proceedings. Did Jenny say much to you?"

"She told me they'd argued and reconciled recently, but not what the argument was about. She said her husband used his fists," Henry said. "We didn't have much time to discuss things."

Gerard squeezed Henry's biceps. "I'm sorry."

"Not your fault. Is London okay?"

"She will be," Gerard said. "Once we catch this bastard."

Gerard's cell phone rang. He didn't recognized the caller. "Hello, Anderson and Drummond Security."

"Hello. This is Matthew Jonas. I'm a real estate agent in Wanaka. My client has purchased a home here or at least he's ready to sign the sale and purchase documents. He's a famous author and doesn't want strangers wandering around the property. He wants an idea of how much it will cost to put in security features—lights and cameras plus a security fence. Would you be able to give him a quote?"

"Did someone refer you?" Gerard asked. They hadn't started advertising yet.

"Yes, the owners of the Gilcrest Station recommended you to my client. He's staying there at present," Matthew Jonas said. "Now, are you able to do a quote? The sooner, the better."

Gerard checked his watch. "It will take me three hours to drive to Wanaka. I could meet you or your client at one, if that's suitable."

"Perfect. I'll text you the address. I will meet you at the property at one."

Gerard hung up. "Another job. Just a quote, but the word is getting out."

"What's the job?"

"Property security. Cameras, lights and fencing. He didn't mention inside the property, but I guess it will be clearer once I see the place."

"I'm sorry this is falling on you."

"No problem," Gerard said. "I'm sure it won't be for much longer. Once your name is cleared, things will return to normal." Or as normal as they could be when a shifter lost his mate. It wasn't bloody fair. Most shifters never found their true mate, the being who completed them. To have a true mate murdered, scarcely before the relationship began, must be hell.

"Car coming," Henry said.

Gerard left the room and entered the lounge, so he could peer out the window. The tension slid from his shoulders. Isabella and Leo. He went to answer the door.

"Our man didn't make an appearance," Leo said once the door closed after them. "Not a peep. Felix and Saber saw no one either."

"Come and have a coffee." Gerard led the way into the kitchen and was pleased to see London had emerged. Her eyes bore large shadows beneath them, and she was pale, but she smiled. He winked in return, relieved she'd picked herself up after last night. He'd worried about her.

"So what's the plan?" Leo asked. "Should we stake out the place tonight?"

"I can't," Isabella said. "I've got my practice self-defense class tonight—the one for Emily and our friends. Are you still coming, London? I need someone with experience to help out."

"I'll be there," London said. "Although I don't know that I'd call myself experienced. I've taken two different classes in Bath."

"I can keep an eye on the house again tonight," Leo offered. "The idea of him out there, taunting London. He needs to be stopped."

"We'll stop him." Henry straightened from his slouch against the counter. "He'll make a mistake soon."

"He will," Isabella agreed.

London sighed. "I hope so. I can't take much more, this looking over my shoulder."

"Fancy time away from Middlemarch? I've got to go to Wanaka to do a quote. Wanna come with me?"

She nodded. "Jenny and I didn't have time to visit Wanaka. I've heard the lake is pretty."

"Once I've done the quote we can spend a few hours sightseeing. They've filmed movies there. You know. Those ones with the elves," Gerard said.

London glanced at him, the corners of her mouth curling up in an almost smile. "You'd better not say that to movie fans. Those movies were popular."

"Not my thing," Gerard said, after everyone finished laughing at him. He didn't care, though, because London looked brighter. He'd do anything to make her happy.

"You have such beautiful scenery in New Zealand." They drove past farmland and vineyards, rivers and small country towns on the way to Wanaka, the tourist town on the banks of a lake by the same name.

She pulled her attention from the scenery to study Gerard. Since last night he'd been so good to her, yet a part of her felt embarrassed by both her behavior and the fact she'd allowed herself to become a victim. She'd known she should have broken off the relationship with Royce earlier. She'd even sensed there had been someone else, but she'd never considered her sister as the other woman since work commitments had kept her away so often.

"None of this is your fault." Gerard's hand landed on hers and squeezed.

"Are you a mind-reader and a hero?"

"I'm an ordinary man."

She sniffed. "There is nothing ordinary about you, Gerard Drummond. You're a special man."

"Once this is over, we'll go on holiday. One of the Pacific Islands. How does that sound?"

"What about your business?"

"Henry has been asking his stepfather to visit ever since we arrived here. If he has to fill in for me for two weeks, he might actually come. I know that would please Henry. He needs his family and his friends around him now."

"I'd love a holiday in the sunshine. I've always wanted to go to a tropical island. Tell me which one," she said. "Give me something to look forward to."

Gerard returned his hand to the steering wheel as they reached the outskirts of Wanaka. "Me too. We could go to Fiji or Western Samoa or Rarotonga. We'll check out the internet when we're home in Middlemarch. I love the idea of seeing you in a bikini."

"Don't own one. I-everyone told me I was too big to wear a bikini."

"Bullshit," Gerard said. "You have seriously sexy curves that will rock a bikini. The only thing we'll need to be careful of is not getting your pale skin sunburned." He grinned and his eyes drifted toward feline. "I can't wait to rub lotion on you. It won't be a hardship."

"Sounds lovely."

"We could even get married over there."

Her lips parted. No, *no*, she was actually gaping. She pressed her lips together and stared at him.

"Too soon? I wanted you to know the direction of my thoughts. I want you for my mate. You know that. Since you're human, you'll want marriage. It's the human way."

"Don't felines get married?"

"Not all the time. If both parties are feline, they can mark each other and that process is tighter than marriage vows."

"I'll think about it."

"I'm fine with that," Gerard said. "This is the right street. The impression the real estate agent gave me was that the house was private and at the end of a long driveway. You going to act as my office assistant again?"

"Sure. The quicker we get this done, the longer we'll have to sightsee. Is the real estate agent meeting us here?"

"So he said." He drove around a bend and the house came into view. A silver Mercedes sedan sat in front of the house. "That must be him. The notebook and pen are on the rear seat."

"Where is he?"

"The front door is open. He must be inside."

They climbed from the SUV and approached the front door.

"Hello," Gerard called. "Anyone there?"

"In here," a masculine voice called.

Gerard headed toward the voice and London trailed him. He stalked through the door and disappeared. London hurried to catch up. She heard a thump, darted through the door and came to an abrupt halt. Gerard lay on the floor, still, and she could see blood trickling down his face.

Royce stood over him, a smirk twisting his expression. "Hello, sweetheart. Bet you didn't expect to see me."

London took two quick steps back, blinking, even though she'd expected Royce, sensed she'd been right to fear he was the one who killed Jenny. "Y-you killed Jenny."

"The bitch owed me."

"*You killed her.*"

"She wanted a divorce. Bitch thought she could click her fingers and get rid of me, thought she could keep her money. After all I went through."

London pressed her hand to her mouth and inched away. Gerard wasn't moving. Her gaze returned to Royce. He'd dropped weight, his face was leaner than she remembered, the furrow between his brows and the ones bracketing his mouth more obvious than when she'd last seen him.

"If she hadn't opened her mouth, she wouldn't have died, but the bitch told me she'd changed her will. Told me and laughed, so I shoved the knife in her chest. Just wanted to scare her, but the bitch *laughed* at me."

London's gaze darted to the door they'd entered, and she whirled, making a run for it. Not quick enough. He seized her, one hand branding her upper arm, and the other fisted in her ponytail.

"I have nothing you need," she gritted out, tears of pain overflowing, splashing her cheeks.

He hauled her around to face him, his cheeks and jaws mottled with anger. He pushed his face close to hers. "Bitch told me she'd left everything to you. If I get rid of you, I won't have a problem."

A horn blared from her jacket pocket, the booming sound making her jump. "It's my friend. She's expecting me to call."

Confidence oozed from him. Entitlement. And it pissed her off. Anger spilled through her, a whoosh of fiery heat and resentment. She might have been a victim once, but no longer. Royce released his grip a fraction to grope in her pocket, turning her body so she faced away from him and it was easier for him to grab her phone.

The relaxation of his guard.

Idiot.

She wasn't the same mouse he'd raped. The classes she'd taken in Bath flew through her mind like a slow-moving movie. She gripped his forearms and dropped her weight downward, taking him by surprise. The instant she had her balance, she stomped on his foot, hard. He shouted, his weight hunching forward as pain took control. She shoved back her elbow, shouting when it connected with his cheekbone.

Yes! Royce seemed stunned by her boldness. Encouraged, her second sharp jab landed a blow on his nose. A sharp crunch sounded as something broke. Royce howled but London didn't wait to assess the damage.

Where was her phone? She scanned the floor and couldn't see it. Instead of searching, she took off for the door, sprinting along the carpeted passage and outside, each breath clawing up her throat and bursting free in a hoarse gasp.

Help.

Royce wouldn't give up that easily.

She needed help.

A red SUV pulled up, and a man dressed in a navy-blue suit climbed from the driver's side. He gaped at her.

"Call the cops!" she screamed, still running. "He's got a gun."

To her horror, the man shut his door and walked toward her, an uncertain smile fading in and out of his expression.

A loud bellow rang out behind her, a feline snarl. She glanced over her shoulder and saw Royce in the doorway. Huh! She'd made his nose bleed. Good job.

Royce skidded to a halt. "Grab her! The woman is insane. She attacked me. Hurry up, man." He swiped blood from his face. "Before she injures you too."

London gaped as the new arrival backed toward his vehicle. "Don't listen to him," she screeched, incensed at Royce.

Bastard.

He still thought he could get away with killing Jenny.

"He murdered my sister. He's wanted by the Middlemarch police. Ring them if you don't believe me."

"The cops are on their way," the new arrival shouted. London assumed it was the real estate agent. The elderly man darted the remaining distance to his vehicle.

"You didn't ring them," Royce said, his manner confident. "I saw you arrive. Run away, old man, and let me deal with this delusional woman."

"Call the cops," London shrieked, poised to flee if Royce came any closer. "Idiot. He's gonna kill you too." Sugar, was Gerard okay? He'd looked...dead. A sob tore at her throat, but she refused to crumple into victim again.

The real estate man started his vehicle, backed up, then floored his accelerator. His SUV fishtailed and roared like an angry beast before gaining traction on the gravel surface and shooting down the driveway.

Sugar, *please* let him call the cops, if he hadn't already.

"What are you gonna do now, London?" Royce taunted her, strolling toward her as if he had all the time in the world.

"You murdered Jenny."

"Your point?" His arrogant smirk held confidence, and he kept edging closer.

She couldn't let him grab her again. She'd been lucky last time and wouldn't take him unawares again.

A feline snarl erupted from the house.

"What the hell?" Royce demanded, his gaze divided between her and the doorway of the property.

Hope surged in London as Gerard appeared in the doorway. His T-shirt hung in tatters around his glossy chest. The fur along his spine stood to attention.

Royce took half a step back while London circled around, ready to offer aid. She picked up a fist-size stone from the edge of the gravel area, feeling better for the weapon.

Royce glanced at her or where she'd been when he last saw her. He swiveled until she was in his sight again. "Where did he come from? You see it?"

Gerard sprang, sending Royce sprawling forward. Royce landed heavily on the gravel and grunted at the impact. He groaned and struggled to his feet.

Gerard watched him with an unblinking stare.

Royce's gaze fastened on her, and he lumbered toward her, determination etched into his expression. Blood trickled down his cheek, and the knee of his black trousers bore a rip. "Bitch. Ya got me so angry, I'm seeing things."

Without a second thought, London fired her rock at Royce. It struck his shoulder with a thunk, and he cried out. London seized the opportunity and jumped at him, shoving him hard with all her might. Off balance, he fell to the ground.

In the distance, the screech of sirens carried on the air, coming in their direction. Thank goodness.

Gerard barked out a growl—a clear demand for her to back off. She retreated, and Gerard disappeared into the house. Royce picked himself up, snarling and sounding more like a beast than Gerard. Keeping her eyes on him, she back-pedaled.

He cackled, an edge of madness to the humor. "Can't escape me. I'm gonna catch you and stick you with a knife, just like your bitch of a sister."

The sirens came closer and closer, and London turned and fled toward them. Her arms and legs pumped, fear propelling her to speed. She spotted the first car and kept sprinting. Royce hurled curses from behind, getting closer but not near enough to grab her.

The cop car skidded to a halt, almost hitting her. She jumped out of the way, sprawling forward as her ankle rolled. She fell face-forward and Royce was on her, punching her head, raining blows on her jaw, her shoulders.

Terror left her lightheaded, the repeated punches causing starbursts behind her eyes. Then, without warning, the attack stopped, the blows ceased. Her head rang. A coppery taste filled her mouth.

"English, are you okay?" Gerard was there, his breathing harsh as he lifted her to her feet.

"Gerard." She lifted a heavy hand, fingers probing the gash on his head.

"I'm fine, or I will be. We're talking about you."

"Move away from her," a harsh voice ordered.

She turned too fast and wavered on her feet, suddenly dizzy. "Gerard is my boyfriend. He has done nothing wrong. Royce attacked him too. He hit Gerard over the head."

Another cop approached from a second car, this one older, his bearing indicating more experience. "Hands where I can see them."

The real estate agent returned, worry written over his face. "Is the house interior damaged? I'm responsible. The owner wants it sold, and I promised to do that."

"Sir," the policeman said in a terse voice. "Please stand back. One of the other officers will speak to you in a moment. I'll get an officer to call the Wanaka Medical Center. Get someone to treat your injuries."

"I want to go home," London said.

"You're bleeding," the cop retorted.

"She attacked me," Royce hollered.

"No, I—"

The policeman halted London's denial. "Once we get you both checked out, we'll take your statements at the police station."

Half an hour later, with their wounds treated and photographed for evidence, the policeman questioned them individually.

London told the policeman about Jenny's murder, that Royce beat and raped her all those years ago and married her sister. The change of will and the zombie run. She told him how the Middlemarch cops had arrested Henry, about the notes she'd received and finally, the events of today. She made a mental note to contact the real estate agent about retrieving her phone.

"Royce admitted to murdering Jenny," she told the policeman. "He told me he did it. He did it because he wanted Jenny's money. He's been following me, waiting for an opportunity to kill me too."

"He told you that?" The policeman sounded doubtful.

"Rumor is he has debts and needs Jenny's money to pay them off. You could contact my sister's solicitor for confirmation." She resettled on the uncomfortable wooden chair in the interview room. Why did these rooms have to be so uninspiring? She felt as if she were drowning in beige. "Will he be charged with my sister's murder?"

"I'm not in charge, but it's looking that way."

The policeman asked several more questions, took notes and got London to sign her statement.

Then, she waited in another room. At least this one had several posters on the wall. Gerard joined her ten minutes later, and they waited some more. It was three hours later when a policeman joined them.

"You can leave now," he said.

London jumped to her feet. "What about Royce?"

"He has been arrested for the murder of Jenny Weaver and on one account of assault with further charges pending."

"Gerard." London clutched his arm.

"Come on, English. Let's go home."

261

They walked from the police station. London suppressed her urge to skip and cheer, relief that the police had captured and charged Jenny's murderer a weight off her shoulders. "I can't believe it's over, that they've arrested Royce for Jenny's murder. What will happen to Henry?"

"I think he'll turn himself in and get his name cleared. We'll talk to Saber and the Feline council and ask how they want to handle the situation."

"You might even be able to file an official complaint regarding the local cops because they didn't have any evidence against Henry and refused to listen to anything I told them. Are you okay to drive?"

Gerard slipped his hand around her waist and guided her to the car. "My head is hard, and the wound has almost knitted together. How do you feel?"

"Relieved. The doctor said I'd have a few aches and pains tomorrow, but I'm so pleased this is over, and soon, I can hold Jenny's funeral. I want to move on and get back to normal."

"We'll do that, English. I'm looking forward to normal."

"Me too." The words were emphatic.

"I'm looking forward to the future too. You'll stay in Middlemarch with me, won't you?"

She smiled at him, caught the faint anxious lines on his brow. "I'm staying."

"With me?"

"Yes, if you want me."

"I want you," he said. "We will get married at the beach on a tropical island."

"It's manners to ask a woman to marry you first."

"I will," he said. "I want to surprise you. Give our lives a chance to revert to normal." He opened the car door for her, waited until she climbed inside and leaned over to kiss her cheek. He pulled back and shut the door before rounding the SUV and climbing into the driver's seat. "Will that work for you?"

"Yes," London said. "Sounds perfect."

Chapter 14

Looking to the Future

One week later

L ife in Middlemarch felt right. London glanced around the faces of people who had become friends. Yesterday, they'd supported her at Jenny's funeral and now they were celebrating the official opening of Isabella's Martial Arts and Self-Defense School.

This country town had become home. Her gaze slid to Gerard, who was standing with Henry and Leo Mitchell. Henry had been pardoned by the Middlemarch police and local gossip said PC Hannah had received an official censure from the cops in charge of the Southern region.

Rumors flew from person to person regarding a possible replacement. No one knew if the gossip held truth.

Gerard sensed her scrutiny and his slow, charming grin did things to her insides. Happiness turned her gaze misty. She loved him. It was that simple.

She wove through the crowds of excited children and gossiping locals, both shifter and human, to reach his side.

"What?" he asked.

"I love you. Will you marry me?"

Gerard let out a whoop. He seized her and dragged her closer, his lips claiming hers. He kissed her until hunger and passion consumed her. She was vaguely aware of cheers and applause, and when Gerard relaxed his hold, she pulled back to find them the center of attention.

"Yes," Gerard whispered in her ear. "I love you too, English."

She reached for his hand and squeezed it while desire and love filled her, body and soul. "Gerard and I are getting married."

The crowd applauded and cheered anew.

"When? Where?" Agnes Paisley asked in her querulous voice. For once, a smile softened her stern face.

Gerard had told her more of the Feline council and how they ran the community. She knew Agnes was a council member.

"We're getting married in Fiji," Gerard said.

There were groans and protests.

"But we will have a celebratory party here once we get home," Gerard said.

"You should get married here," Isabella said, appearing in front of them.

"No," Gerard said. "We have decided on a beach wedding."

Isabella turned to Leo. "We're going to Fiji. Can you arrange time off work?"

London exchanged a laughing look with Gerard, a slight nod. "All right. You and Leo and Henry—if he wants—can come to our wedding."

"I hate flying," Leo grumbled.

"We'll drug you," Isabella said. "Just imagine. We'll get to have a holiday in the warm. Warm weather and bikinis."

Leo sighed. "I'll take the drugs, sweetheart. You're right."

"We're going home," Gerard said. "To celebrate."

Isabella opened her mouth and closed it. She nodded. "Thanks for coming to my opening and helping me with the self-defense demo."

"You're welcome," London said.

"We'll let you know dates," Gerard said, "but it will be soon."

London nodded. They might have had a quick courtship, but she was sure in her mind about her future. "Let's go home."

A short drive later, they walked into Henry and Gerard's house. Geoffrey barked at them, then placed his head on his paws to wait for Henry's arrival.

Gerard took her hand and led her to their bedroom. "I love you, London." He walked to the wardrobe and pulled something from a pocket in his leather jacket. He turned around to face her. "I bought this for you last week when Henry and I had to go to Dunedin." He opened the small box to reveal an emerald-and-diamond engagement ring. His smile was wide and bright as he lifted the ring from its protective box and reached for her hand. Joy blazed on his face, in his eyes, dug into his cheeks to produce cute dimples. "I wanted to make everything official."

"Yes," she whispered, her throat tight with emotion.

"I love you, London Allbright. Knowing you return my love makes me the happiest shifter alive." He pushed the ring onto her finger, and they both grinned.

"We should celebrate in the feline way too," London said. "I love you, Gerard. In the past I would've worried I didn't know you. Not now. I've never felt so confident of a decision."

"Come here," he whispered, his tone gritty with the same emotion that tightened her throat.

She went willingly, let him peel off her clothes and press her onto the mattress. He released her to strip off his clothes then returned with a grin. Their arms wrapped around each other, and they kissed, celebrating their love. His breath caressed her face, his fingers relearned her body. Soon that wasn't enough. She parted her thighs, her hips canting upward in invitation. She was wet for him, craving his possession. Gerard notched his cock to her entrance, and they both groaned as he entered her. His hands skimmed with purpose, with skill, teasing and pushing her higher.

Their kisses moved from sweet and slow to demanding and passionate, each sweep of his tongue pushing the pulse at her throat to beat a rapid tattoo. Her breaths came in gasps, passion rising between them until she drowned in the desire.

Her pussy clenched around his cock as he licked her mating site. His tongue laved to and fro, then just as she flew in climax, Gerard sank his teeth deep. She groaned, pain and pleasure warring, the twists of sensation almost too much for her to handle.

Long seconds later, Gerard lifted his head and licked the wound. Each delicate lap of his tongue had heat blossoming, renewed pleasure writhing over her nerve endings.

She kissed Gerard's neck, instinct guiding her to his marking site. Although he'd told her he didn't need a bite, that they'd still be mates, she wanted to mark him in passion. Instinct drove her, and she bit Gerard, glorying in his dark groan, the shudder that went through his big body. On tasting blood, she lifted her head. *Eew. She hadn't meant to draw blood.* She tried to lift her head.

"Lick it clean," Gerard ordered, and she obeyed.

The coppery taste wasn't so bad.

He trembled and his hips stilled, leaving him embedded inside her. She felt the contractions of his shaft as he came, and was glad she'd visited Gavin, the feline doctor, for a birth control shot. Sex was better without a condom.

He cupped the back of her head with his hand and lifted it to kiss her. She felt the passion in him, the love in each of his caresses. His kiss inflamed, it consumed as he plundered her mouth.

When he gentled the kiss, they were both breathing hard. He withdrew from her body and smiled at her, his gaze going to the spot where he'd bitten her. He tapped her new mark, and she jumped at the spike of heat. Her nipples puckered, and a purr issued from Gerard.

"I'd heard the spot was sensitive." He fingered the spot again. "I love seeing my mark on you."

"Will it always be there?"

"Yes. It will only fade if I die."

She gripped his ears and forced him to look at her. "You're not going to do that, are you?"

"Not in the near future."

"Good." She frowned. "I didn't think I could leave a mark on you. There is a small raised area."

"I hoped that would be the case," he said and satisfaction rippled in him. "All the human-feline pairings who live in Middlemarch or came from here bear marks. Both parties."

"What does it mean?"

"That we're true mates," Gerard said. "We're perfect together and meant to be."

A heady sense of satisfaction filled her as she watched him, saw his enjoyment of the moment. "I love the sound of that."

"We'll get married as soon as we can book our holiday."

"Perfect."

"Happy ever after, English," he said, his grin wide and toothy. "Happy ever after."

Yes, she thought. Middlemarch was a good community, and she was happy, so happy here. With Gerard at her side, life couldn't get any sweeter.

Chapter 15

Feline Shapeshifter Council Meeting.

Mitchell Farm, Middlemarch, New Zealand

Present Saber Mitchell, Sid Blackburn, Kenneth Nesbitt, Agnes Paisley, Valerie McClintock, Benjamin Urquart

"There is a certain part of the community who are against mixed marriages and their rumblings are becoming louder." Valerie removed her glasses and refused to look at Saber, instead wiping them with a lenses cloth. "I've had several feline families contact me to express their concern at the rising number of humans trusted with our secret."

Rage roared through Saber. His mate was a human, and she supported the feline community with everything she possessed. "My mate is a human. Gerard's mate is a human, and the way I hear it, Henry's mate was also a human."

"Henry is a werewolf," Agnes retorted, her prune expression of disapproval anchored in heavy wrinkles. "That is another concern with members. Henry Anderson's application to bring his stepfather into the community has raised several objections. They're saying, quite rightly, that Henry was in jail for a serious crime and—"

"The man was jailed by our incompetent cops," Kenneth said, his face florid with indignation. "You should stand up for the werewolf. Why are they concerned when Henry has done nothing wrong? They should worry more about our two lazy cops who do a crap job for our town."

"Tell me the rumors of a replacement are true," Ben said.

Saber confined his thoughts to himself. The less he said, the better, although his feline stalked his mind, and his claws protruded, pricking his clenched palms. If he discovered who was causing trouble, he might take matters into his own hands. He'd married Emily—a human.

Gerard had mated with London, and Marsh had a human mate. Who the devil was singling them out?

Sid picked up his mug of tea, took a sip and set it down with a click. "The lad has a right to be angry. Emily is an excellent addition to our town, as are the other human mates who have integrated into our group. What is going on, Valerie? Why have people started complaining? The humans bring new genes to our feline bloodlines. The resulting children are feline. Why are the felines anti-human?"

Ben reached for a piece of shortbread and crunched on the crisp cookie. He swallowed, his brow scrunched in a frown. "The rumors I've been hearing are that people aren't enjoying the changes we've introduced. They prefer the old ways—our community remaining isolated."

Saber snorted. "We can't live like that any longer. We have to move with the times. Many of the families have commented favorably of their children returning to take part in the events we've organized. We have new businesses starting in Middlemarch. The market gives locals a way to make money from their arts and crafts."

"Lad." Sid patted Saber's hand. "No one is getting at you."

"They're not? What is going on then?" It sure as hell felt as if he stood in the spotlight.

"Some felines think you're too young to be on the council, and that you're leading us in the wrong direction," Ben said.

"No one wanted to take Uncle Herbert's spot on the council," Saber said, working to keep his voice even. "I'd be happy to relinquish my spot if someone else wants to volunteer."

"No," Valerie said.

"No." Agnes was more emphatic.

"I agree with the ladies," Kenneth said. "You do a stellar job. We needed you—someone younger on the council to be creative."

"Then why is there a problem?" Saber demanded.

"Human—I mean, feline nature," Sid said. "How about this? Next time we hold a general feline meeting, we'll ask for ideas of how to move forward. Fund-raising solutions, ideas to improve our community, get everyone to air their concerns. For those who make sensible suggestions, ones that might help our town, we'll give them a temporary seat on the council while we implement their ideas. That way, those who are interested or who complain regarding the way we're doing things now, will have a chance to take action. What do you think? Will that work?"

"You always get people who complain but they aren't willing to help either," Agnes said. "Pass the shortbread please."

Saber passed her the plate. "That's sneaky. We're making concessions but expect those complaining to help."

"Huh!" Kenneth wiped the perspiration off his forehead. "I bet our complainers won't want to put their money where their mouths are."

"We'll see," Sid said, his faded green eyes twinkling.

"What are we going to work on for our next event?" Valerie asked. "I admit I was skeptical about our plans at first, but I'm liking the civic spirit that is growing in the town."

"We will organize another zombie run for the spring since we promised those who weren't able to finish discounted entry," Agnes said. "Everyone who participated said how much they enjoyed the race. I suppose we could hold another dance."

"Emily mentioned something this morning," Saber said. He wondered if he should bother with the suggestion, given the petty mindedness of some.

"Out with it, lad," Sid commanded. "Emily has offered excellent suggestions so far."

"Emily likes to read. She reads romances and mysteries on her e-reader." Not one of the council made a snide comment, so Saber continued. "One series she likes is set in an imaginary town where they advertise Halloween for the entire year. Emily suggested we take this idea and make it our own. Make a haunted house for the week before Halloween. People will pay to be scared. She suggested that everyone dress up in costumes and we give a prize for the best one. We can arrange trick or treating for the younger children and have a separate costume prize for them too."

"Excellent idea," Agnes said, nodded hard enough to make her stiff curls bob.

"Emily suggested we use the old house on the Dewhurst property. It's a large house with lots of different rooms. We can patch the rain damage and the walls damaged by vandals. It should be easy enough," Saber said.

"I think that is a marvelous idea," Valerie said. "We can use sound effects and go all out, perhaps using our special feline qualities to scare humans. I vote yes."

Sid nodded approval, and Saber relaxed. Once Sid was behind an idea, the rest of the council agreed.

"I like the other plan too," Sid said. "Let's put this idea to a feline meeting and ask them to come up with additional ideas."

"Anyone over thirty is eligible to suggest an idea and sit on the council temporarily," Valerie said.

"No." Saber glanced around the circle of familiar faces. "Anyone who can shift may put forward their ideas and get a temporary seat. That's fairer and will involve everyone."

"Outrageous," Agnes snapped. "Young felines have no good sense. May I remind you it was the problems with our youngsters that sent us on this path to start with?"

"No, if we do this, it needs to be fair for everyone, no matter their age," Saber insisted.

"Lad is right," Ben said. "Everyone should have equal opportunity."

Sid tapped a pen on his note pad. "The human mates should have the same opportunity."

"I agree," Saber said. "Emily and Caroline have already contributed to our successful functions."

"I second that," Kenneth said, surprising Saber since he usually sided with Agnes and Valerie.

"Are we agreed?" Sid glanced at Agnes then Valerie. Both women nodded. "We're decided then. The next general meeting is after the upcoming rodeo. Let's keep this under our hats until the meeting. A show of hands."

Saber lifted his hand, then Kenneth and Ben and finally Agnes and Valerie.

"Agreed," Sid said with satisfaction. "That's it, I think." He glanced at his watch. "Perfect timing. I must be off. We have visitors for dinner." He stood and the others rose to leave.

Saber followed them out and waved goodbye. They didn't seem too bothered about the growing dissension in the community. He'd keep an ear out for rumbles, and if he heard anyone badmouthing Emily, there would be a ruckus, followed by his fist.

About Author

USA Today bestselling author Shelley Munro lives in Auckland, the City of Sails, with her husband and a cheeky Jack Russell/mystery breed dog.

Typical New Zealanders, Shelley and her husband left home for their big OE soon after they married (translation of New Zealand speak - big overseas experience). A twelve-month-long adventure lengthened to six years of roaming the world. Enduring memories include being almost sat on by a mountain gorilla in Rwanda, lazing on white sandy beaches in India, whale watching in Alaska, searching for leprechauns in Ireland, and dealing with ghosts in an English pub.

While travel is still a big attraction, these days Shelley is most likely found in front of her computer following another love - that of writing stories of contemporary and paranormal romance and adventure. Other interests include watching rugby (strictly for research purposes), cycling, playing croquet and the ukelele, and curling up with an enjoyable book.

Visit Shelley at her Website
www.shelleymunro.com

Join Shelley's Newsletter
www.shelleymunro.com/newsletter

Visit Shelley's Facebook page
www.facebook.com/ShelleyMunroAuthor

Follow Shelley at Bookbub
www.bookbub.com/authors/shelley-munro

Also By Shelley

Paranormal

Middlemarch Shifters
My Scarlet Woman
My Younger Lover
My Peeping Tom
My Assassin
My Estranged Lover
My Feline Protector
My Determined Suitor
My Cat Burglar
My Stray Cat
My Second Chance
My Plan B
My Cat Nap
My Romantic Tangle

My Blue Lady
My Twin Trouble
My Precious Gift

Middlemarch Gathering

My Highland Mate
My Highland Fling

Middlemarch Capture

Snared by Saber
Favored by Felix
Lost with Leo
Spellbound with Sly
Journey with Joe
Star-Crossed with Scarlett

www.ingramcontent.com/pod-product-compliance
Lightning Source LLC
Chambersburg PA
CBHW052030240626
47153CB00006B/2033